# A SEA OF SORROW AND SCORN

## THE LEVANTHRIA SERIES

## A.P. BESWICK

A.P. BESWICK PUBLICATIONS

*This book was crowd funded through Kickstarter. To everyone who has helped me to turn a dream into reality, thank you.*

***The Captains Tier***

*Ellen Pilcher*
*Mat Meillier*

*To my youngest daughter Etta who coined the best pirate insult I have heard, which I had to include in this story - Boo Slugger! She is also the inspiration behind the character Esara.*

# THE LEGENDARY PIECES OF EIGHT

**To the legends of the ocean who backed the highest tier.
I salute you.**

**Seth (Blackbeard) Alexander
Z (The Sparrow)**

# TO THE MERRY MEN... AND WOMEN

To the legends that backed the highest tier in A Forest Of Vanity And Valour

**Seth (The Little) Alexander**
**Joshua (The Scarlett) Grey**
**Daniel (The Friar) Dorman**
**Robin (The Hood) Hill**

Forest of Opiya

Pendaren H

Eltera

Gondoron Pass

Osar

Askela

Och Bragoa

# Levanthria

Usterian plains

Uster

ntar

Pugo's Tears

N

Rivah

Voraz

Zakron Keep

# I

## ZERINA

'Bring them to heel, bring them to me. The King has decreed that all magic casters surrender themselves to aid in the war effort. Either they join us and help win this war or their fate will be sealed in open court for contempt.'
*Morgana dressing the Royal Court- 261 KR*

On a cold stone floor, with my knees tucked up to my chest, I shiver. I have been kept separate from my sisters since our capture, and now find myself awaiting trial for a crime I did not commit. Magic may run through my blood, but until the night of our capture, I did not know it could be used in such a devastating way. I have worried every day since what fate awaits my sister, Briasse, for the injuries she caused.

After two days without food or water, exhaustion creeps in, but I do not wish to close my eyes in such a dark place. How would I protect myself from the guards who creep outside my door?

The clink of metal startles me and my head bolts

upright. A man carries a torch in one hand as he unlocks the gates to my own personal hellspace.

I recognize him at once: it is the man who led my sisters' and my capture, who read our charges of witchcraft. His dark hair is slicked back under his squared hat, and his pointed smile makes my nerves peak.

"Have you made your decision, witch?" he says as he steps inside the cell. There is a venom in the way he speaks, an air of disgust on his face while he addresses me. "Will you join the ranks of mages that are being recruited for the King's War, or will you stand trial for the crimes you and your sisters have committed?"

I do not wish to speak to this vile man who has destroyed the peaceful life that my sisters and I have lived for so long, alone in the hilltops. I spit in his direction, and it lands just short of his pristinely polished boots.

His face turns into a smile, and he rushes me, grabbing me by my arms and dragging me to my feet. I am too weak to fight back, and he pins me against the wall, then brings his mouth close to my ear.

"Listen, witch. If I had my way, you would not be of this earth right now. The crown offers you a kindness. It would do you well to accept this offer with some gratitude." The growl in his voice vibrates through my body and fills me with fear, and I do not understand his hatred.

I have every reason to hate him, however; he has torn me from my home, from my sisters, and now makes threats to our lives like the three of us mean nothing.

"Show *gratitude*?" I snap. "Live the life of a slave fighting in a war I do not believe in, or greet death?"

An angry burst of energy fires up from within me, and I flick my head to the side as hard as I can, making contact with the side of his face. My ears begin to ring. I have never hurt anyone before but for what this man has done, I enjoy this moment. The force knocks the hat from his head and he jumps back, his eyes darkened and face red.

He raises his hand and strikes me across the face, knocking me back into the wall. He steps forward and grabs my hair, then slams my head against the stone wall behind me. The small cell spins wildly and I drop to my knees in a daze, but I cannot help but force a smile at being able to cause him some damage. I no longer care if I will regret it.

"Stupid girl," the man growls as he picks his hat from the floor.

"What have you done with my sisters?" I mumble through the fog that comes with a blow to the head.

"They are to stand trial, as are you," he snarls. "Your elder sister has not been given the option of clemency. She has shown how dangerous her magic truly is. Her fate is already sealed."

Briasse's power was something I did not know was possible. When the mob came to our door, she wielded fire from her hands as if she controlled it, manipulated it.

"She was trying to protect us from *you*," I answer. Briasse was doing what she had always done: sheltering us from the outside world. She knew the magic she wielded was destructive, yet she shielded us from it by helping us to live a life in solitude.

"And what makes your lives inherently more valuable than the men and women that now carry burns for the rest of their lives?"

"It was you and your men that attended our house uninvited, carrying weapons and torches."

"You are witches. I am merely holding up the law at the request of the king and the sorceress, Morgana." It almost seems that a flicker of regret passes across his face.

I have not heard of this Morgana, but if she is the cause of the violence we have endured, she will have to pay the price. Why would a sorceress wish to inflict this kind of suffering on her kin?

The man crouches down and brings his face towards mine. He runs the back of his hand down my cheek, following the tears that run down my face. "You are vile, unnatural creatures," he whispers. Spit leaves his mouth as he dresses me down, and a chill streams down my spine.

I have not felt fear like this in a long time. Not since seeing Lyrissa's broken body as the magic use wore her down. With the hatred in his eyes, I can't help but wonder if I am to make it to the trials at all, or if he will end my life here in this cell.

"Please don't do this, I beg – " he strikes me across the face, knocking me onto my side. I wipe blood from the corner of my mouth. "Please at least allow me to see my sisters."

"I am not a monster." He tilts my chin up to meet his eyes, and smiles.

His stubbled face greets mine, and I wonder what happened to him for him to show such hatred towards me, a stranger. "I will allow you to see your sisters for a few moments before you stand trial. But heed my warning: should I suspect a single spark of magic from any of you, I will have you all tortured for days in front of the entire kingdom. In your final moments you will beg for the kindness that death will bring." He gets up and directs his attention to the door. "Take her to her sisters. She has made her decision. She will stand trial with the others."

My vision is blurred but I can make out two figures as they rush into the room, and I feel a pressure under my arms where they take hold of me. My hands are bound behind my back, and I am marched forward. I stumble, still dizzy from my assault, and lose my footing. The guards do not allow me to find my feet, and I am dragged across the stone floor. The only reprieve is that I will be able to see my sisters.

That no matter what fate lies ahead, I will have them both by my side.

We stop a few cells down from my own, and the sound of keys jangling causes me to lift my head and focus on my surroundings. The lock clicks and the squeak of large metal bolts causes my heart to jolt.

"Briasse? Lyrissa?" Pained words leave my mouth as I call out for my sisters, needing to see them.

"Sister?" Briasse struggles to form words from her swollen face. The beating she received is no doubt punishment for her fight. Her arms are in clamps, fastened above her head against the stone walls of her cell. Her black dress is torn from being dragged here. The jet-black hair we share hangs, unkempt, over her face, matted with sweat and blood.

"Fire consumes us, eats us, it is not bad, it is good. Dark magic they fear, dark magic, yes."

I recognise Lyrissa's mumbled words, brought on by the madness that has engulfed her through her magic use. They have not bound her nor beaten her, most likely because her affliction is clear: her mind has gone, and her body is a broken husk of her once confident self.

"Use it, breathe it, find it," she mutters. I have heard her stutter such words for close to three years now. She no longer succumbs to the addiction that magic use brings, but the damage it has done to her body and her mind is unforgiving. She rocks in the corner of the cell, mumbling broken phrases, drooling over herself, unable to feed,

5

unable to bathe. Her skin is wrinkled and aged, her hair greying as though she were our grandmother and not our sister.

"I am here, Lyrissa," I say, shaking off the guards as I move into the cell. I throw them a stare and wish that I had the power to inflict a curse upon them. I want to reassure her, but she does not seem aware of our dank surroundings or the fate that awaits us. She doesn't acknowledge my words, and she continues to rock in the corner.

"Whatever happens, Zerina, do not show them fear. Do not let them know that they have broken you," Briasse tells me. Even in her condition she still stands tall against our oppressors.

"I *am* afraid though," I choke on my words as they form.

"It is fated, fated yes, the gods they have a plan. A plan, a plan." Lyrissa's mumblings grow louder, and she begins to rock faster and faster.

"That's enough!" the man commands, and I am hoisted back through the doorway by clawing hands.

The dirt and stone graze the tops of my feet. It does not take long before I am dragged from the darkness, the brightness of the light outside blinding me.

The noise that greets me is one which I am not expecting. It is as if the hatred the man shows me has been intensified a hundred times over. Scores of people stand outside, booing and screaming at me, and the deafening noise amplifies my disorientation. There is a dull thud against my body, and as I stare down at the floor, I see the blurred remnants of rotten cabbage.

"Burn her!"

"Remove her head!"

"Witch scum!"

Men, women, and children line the streets, hurtling

profanities and threats at me. My vision slowly returns to me and I glance over my shoulder to see my sisters also being dragged out in front of the baying crowd. There are others, too, lined up and paraded in front of everyone as they await their trials.

I fear what is going to happen to us. But I take comfort in the fact that whatever fate awaits us, I will be able to face it with my head held high. With my sisters.

# 2
## ULRIK

The first few days after disembarking from a ship are the hardest. You can find yourself standing in a shop, tavern, or market stall, and suddenly the world around you begins to move. It is a trick of the mind, an illusion, but one which can leave you unsteady on your feet. Your world will begin to move as if you are swaying back and forth, battling the waves you have encountered for many months whilst at sea.

It has been a steady three-day ride as I make my way home to Osar. The weather has been kind to me on my journey. Aside from the odd buck, my steed appears to be tolerant of me. The vendor's son had insisted on giving me plenty of apples to feed him, adamant that the horse would cooperate as long as I spoiled him.

My heart skips when I see the bright evergreen trees that surround Osar, trees I thought I would never see again. All I have thought about for as long as I can remember is being able to see my mother and sister again. To be able to squeeze them tightly and tell them how much I love them. My father, a good man, died before my sister was born, murdered by a thief whilst selling wine at the markets in a nearby city. Unfortunately, goodness does not always favour the kind-hearted.

Exquisite wine production from the rare jarjoba trees that only grow in our region was our family trade, passed down through generations. When my father was murdered, my mother was heavily pregnant, leaving only me to work the vineyard. As hard as I tried, I was too young to carry such a burden, and despite my best efforts, our vineyard found itself in a state of disrepair.

As the trees grow closer, I take in the view of Osar and I cannot help but smile. I have dreamt of this moment for so long, and now I am home. I kick my heels into my horse and we set off at a gallop. He is fast, faster than any horse I have ridden. I have not had much practice since leaving, having been mostly at sea for the past seven years where there is no use for such animal.

The air presses against me and I tense my muscles as I grip the reins tightly so I do not lose balance and fall. If not for the tricorn on my head, I am sure my hair would resemble the horse that I now make my own.

I wonder how my sister has grown. I imagine a little girl with blond locks like our mother, unlike my own dark hair, which I inherited from our father. I was fifteen when I enlisted to work aboard the *Iris*. At age four, she was too young to understand my decision. I can still remember having to peel her hands from my neck as I bid her farewell.

My heart beats quickly and dirt flies through the air as we cover the remaining ground to Osar. I enter through the tall jarjoba trees that surround it. The village looks the same as the day I left. Large pine trees surround the outer edge, and patchwork fields approach full harvest as the farmers ready themselves for the spoils of their hard labour.

Livestock graze within one of the fields where a sow embraces her newfound motherhood as her young press against her belly to suckle from her. This season brings new life and fresh beginnings.

As I steady my horse, I feel nothing but the joy of reuniting with everyone after so long. Moving at a canter, I know that I just need to ride past the first row of houses and take a right, following the street to the bottom. That is here where our family home sits, abutting our old vineyard.

The steady whispers from the older villagers begin. I bring my hand to my tricorn and give a polite nod.

"Is that who I think it is?"

"That's Orson's boy."

"Ulrik is all grown up!"

I smile and tip my head to them as I pass. As much as I would like to make niceties, it is my mother and Esara who I must prioritise.

Two men engaged in conversation pause and bow their heads to me, as if to pay me some form of respect. Kira, an older woman I recognise from the bakery I used to visit as a child, looks as if a creature has just drained the blood from her.

Concerned by the strange looks I am getting, I strike my horse with my heels and we speed up once more through the centre of the village. I make a sharp right turn and our home comes into view. One of the windows is boarded up, the garden fence is broken, and the plants leading up to the pathway look as though they have been trampled.

I drop from the saddle, my ankle stinging when I land too hard.

"Mother? Esara?" I call out as I make my way to the crooked gates that sit disjointed in the small garden fence.

I rush to the door. It opens loosely and I notice that the

frame is splintered. A sign of forced entry. I take a shaky breath and step inside, afraid of what I will discover.

Chairs lie on their sides, and the table is splintered as if something has crashed through it with force. The hairs on my arms stand on end.

I go to the pantry and find it empty, then I rush up the stairs.

"Mother? Esara?" Each time I shout the words again, my voice becomes more and more frantic.

I exit the front of the house and remove my tricorn. I'm too hot, I can't breathe, and I am unsteady on my feet.

"Ulrik? Ulrik my boy, is that you?" It is Gillet, his portly frame still the same as I remember. His hair is grey now, and far more receded than it once was.

"Where is my mother?" I ask him. "Where is Esara?" I do not have time for small talk.

Gillet hesitates, shifting uncomfortably.

"Gillet!" I bark "Where is my family?"

"They – they took them," he stammers.

"Who? Who would take them? Answer me!"

"The guards! They travelled from Eltera and took them away for trial." Gillet bumbles his way through his words.

"Trial?" I feel my body go cold. "What were their crimes, Gillet?"

"Witchcraft! They stand accused of witchcraft."

His words do not make any sense to me. How could the kingdom know of the magic my mother and sister possess?

"They were taken two weeks ago, Ulrik. They stand trial any day now." Gillet can barely look me in the eye.

"No doubt it is the people of this village who accuse my family of such madness." I vault onto my horse and circle him away from the house. "Were you so brave to stand by while they were taken?" I yell. "Or better still, was it you that accused them of this?" But I do not have time to deal with Gillet.

I heel the horse and we set off towards Eltera. These people have sentenced my mother and sister to death. I must do whatever it takes to save them.

# 3
## ZERINA

'This letter grants absolute discharge to one Ulrik Thatch for services to the Kings fleet. Mr Thatch has shown bravery too rarely seen in combat, for this reason his request to return home to his family has been granted.'

*Dicharge notes of Ulrik Thatch - 262 KR*

The crowd bays for our blood. They scream and shout whatever bile they so wish towards us. Lyrissa stands where she is told, and her usual mutterings fall from her mouth. I tremble into myself, my body turned away from the crowd. A cabbage pelts me in the side of the head as I seek to turn, and a wave of rotten vegetables are hurled at us from the roaring crowd.

The degradation is like nothing I have ever experienced. I do not know how Bri doesn't let it affect her. She stands tall and proud, her chin pointed upwards: she will not be broken by these people. Her face is black from the bruising, a bitter gift from our captor.

To the side of us stand the others accused of the same crimes that we are. Most are women, but there is one man. A child stands beside to me, tears streaming down her blackened face, her clothes torn.

How could they force a little girl to endure this? Do these people know nothing of compassion or humility? I presume she is the daughter of the woman next to her. They share similar shaped features and the same blond hair. The mother looks as beaten as Bri, and I can only guess at the fierceness with which she defended her child.

With our mother dead, it was Bri who stood defending us at the end, doing what she could to protect those she loves.

A snivelling man in fine-looking robes appears in front of us, and the crowd draws silent. "You are here today to stand trial," he announces, addressing us all as one. "Your crime is wielding the unnatural powers that magic grants." He has a white, balding head, and his wrinkled skin folds on his forehead.

As our charges are read, we are granted a brief reprieve from the rotten vegetables. All I can hear are the sniffles and sobs of those around us that face these accusations. Mine and the girl's next to me make the most noise.

"Eleven of you stand before us. I will grant you one last chance of clemency. Pledge yourself to the King's War and you will be allowed to live and hone your skills under Morgana." His voice is weathered and hoarse, most likely from calling out loudly at trials such as this.

The man who stands with us clears his throat before speaking. "I do, I pledge myself to the king and to Morgana's ranks."

The crowd boos with displeasure. The weasel in front of

us nods to some guards who make their way forward and drag the man from the stand.

One of the women who stands next to him spits at his back. "Coward!" she snipes, unimpressed with his decision.

How could someone pledge their loyalty to a crown that treats us this way? The man is ushered away by the guards, all the while being threatened by the crowd.

The old man reading our charges raises his hand to settle the mob. They follow commands as if they are pets. So obedient.

"Of the ten that now remain, six of you have already been witnessed to bear magic first-hand whilst being apprehended, injuring guards and people of Levanthria who merely attempt to honour the crown's will. The curse that runs through your body has corrupted your minds and as such, you must be stopped. You are hereby sentenced to death." He nods at the guards again and they rush forward, taking hold of the women that stand around us.

Vomit builds in the back of my throat. Bri used magic against our attackers.

To my left, Bri stands tall and unfazed, choosing not to show fear. A guard steps up behind her and brings a blade to her throat, then slashes from one side to the other.

"Briasse!" My legs buckle. Disbelief overcomes me and I begin to wail.

Blood spills from Bri's throat, spraying the wooden platform where we stand, painting it crimson. The crowd cheers. One by one, the guards execute the other women. No opportunity for last words, no opportunity to say goodbye to loved ones. As Bri drops to her knees, she attempts to speak, but nothing but a gurgle leaves her lips before she falls forward and bleeds to death. The pool of blood grows around her until it begins to drip from the edge of the platform.

I struggle to catch my breath and I begin to fall, but a guard holds my arms firm. My heart is broken.

"Mother!" the girl next to me shrieks. Guards slit the mother's throat whilst she looks into her daughter's eyes one last time. The woman lies on the floor convulsing as her life force leaves her body. Her daughter's hair is no longer the dirty blond it was. Now it is red. The girl is as inconsolable as I am. What monsters treat people this way?

Four of us remain: the girl, an old woman, Lyrissa, and me. We are pushed together with no care for the bodies that lie around us. As the guards parade us around, my feet slip in the pools of blood. The crowd cheers with ecstasy at our dismay. I can no longer hold it in. I vomit on the ground in front of me.

"The four of you that remain will be tested to see if you do in fact possess magic," the old man says. He gives another nod and we are led from the platform.

My poor sister is gone. I am bereft of pain, I feel numb. Briasse brought me up with our father. She was the closest thing to mother I ever had.

What tests do they speak of? If this is to be our fate, I would rather they slit my throat now so that I can join my mother, my father, and now Bri.

# 4

## ULRIK

The gates of Eltera are ginormous. The wrought iron bars are raised, allowing for people to travel freely in and out of the kingdom. The bright white stones that form the wall on the perimeter deflect the sun's light towards me, forcing me to lower my gaze.

I haven't stopped since I left Osar, and my horse begins to slow, growing tired from the journey. If I continue at pace through the Elterian streets, I risk being arrested by the guards, so I slow down just in time as I pass through the gates. The guards who protect the entranceway look me up and down before giving me the nod to pass through.

The long ride has proven tiresome, and I feel as though I have run a length myself. Sweat collects around my face and my clothes are sodden against my skin.

Then my horse stops. Apparently he has chosen to show his stubborn side, and he declines my request to continue our journey. I do not have time for games. I dismount and walk him across the street to an inn where I hitch him to a post. A young girl stands outside, cleaning the area of the rubbish strewn on the ground.

"Keep an eye on my horse, girl. There's coin in it for you," I tell her.

It has been many a year since I stood foot in this city, but I can remember the streets well enough to know where my family will be held. I just pray to the gods that I am not too late. My ride has taken me two hours which is quick for the distance we have covered, but I fear it may not have been quick enough.

The city is quiet, which makes it easier for me to navigate the cobbled streets as I hurry to my destination. My legs ache as I make ground, and my thighs burn, but I must prevail.

It is not long before I see the formed crowds ahead of me. A chorus of cheers echo down the street, a ruckus of delight at whatever it is they see.

The noise grows louder as I approach. The back of the crowd forms a wall off flesh and bone. I peer over the tops of heads, but it is difficult to see, so I push myself through. The feeling is claustrophobic. Bodies compress against me as I fight to see what is happening. People push and kick me in disapproval, but I knock them out of the way.

My eyes widen as I reach the front. I have seen sights that would make any man or woman sick, and I consider myself desensitised to the crueller side of man. But nothing can prepare me for this. The platform just ahead of the crowd is covered in blood, and bodies of women are piled up in front, disregarded and unimportant. From one corner to the other, multiple pikes are protruding from the ground. I feel sick to my stomach as the crown cheers at the sight of an executioner holding up the head of a young woman bereft of her body. A once white cowl is still fixed to her head. Her blood spills from her neck where her body has been detached. The crowd cheers as the executioner makes his way to one of the pikes, then forces the head firmly into place, like a warped trophy.

"Burn them!" one man calls.

"They will curse us from the afterlife!" a woman screams, manic with fear.

If this is how they treat people with magic, they deserve whatever curse they fear, and worse.

The executioner returns to the platform and grabs hold of another victim. He spins, clutching the head in front of him, the long blond hair matted with blood. The mouth is open wide as if she died mid-scream, her eyes open with the realisation of her fate. It is a face that I recognise, one that I can never forget.

It is my mother.

My legs give way, and my knees smash into the cobblestones. My eyes sting as they fill with tears.

My mother is dead, slaughtered without any dignity and paraded like a sick trophy for all these people to cheer and clap. If I had the capability, I would strike every one of them down. They all deserve it, they are all cowards and murderers in my eyes. A large lump forms in my throat as I struggle to process the scene that unfolds before me. Then, anger takes hold.

"Monsters!" I roar, dragging myself back to my feet. The people around me step away, not wishing to be associated with the one voice that sees reason in this madness.


"Esara!" I call out as loud as I can. "Esara! Can you hear me. Are you there?" I panic for my sister's well-being now. I cannot grieve for my mother here, nor can I help her. I can only aim to save Esara from suffering the same fate.

My jaw is clenched and my fists follow suit. When the

executioner slams my mother's head onto the pike, I become a passenger to my rage. These people will bear my wrath.

My chest thunders like the darkest storm, and I rush towards the executioner, who has his back turned to me as he makes his way to the bloodied platform. He has a large build and stands a good foot taller than me. He wears a black gown, and his head is covered to protect his identity.

There are gasps of shock from the people behind me as I throw myself into the back of the gutless murderer. I push him into the platform where he braces himself with his outstretched arms before turning to face me. I am quickly upon him and begin to strike his face multiple times before he pushes me away with force. He steps forward to grab me, but I am too quick for him. Pulling my knife from my side, I step into his hold and feel the small blade tear through his flesh. His eyes open wide and he screams in pain. I force my blade even further, then pull it out and stab him again and again.

The executioner is dead before he hits the floor.

Two more guards run at me and I jump onto the platform to gain the higher ground. Screams of women begin to ring out and I can't help but scoff at their displeasure. The executioner deserved his fate. These women did not.

My mother did not.

# 5

## ZERINA

'*The sisters of Haroosha is a fabled tale from years passed. Three sisters, one tortured and murdered inn keeper. Brought to justice by the fabled monster slayer Gregor.*'

*Jordel Torvin - 255 KR*

My head is brought up from the barrel and I gasp for breath, my hair slapping against my panicked face. Water sprays from my mouth as I cough to clear my lungs, desperate to take in as much air as I can. I have lost count of the number of times I have been submerged into the disgusting black liquid.

"Please stop, I – " my face is forced into the water again. My arms flail wildly. The muffled noises from the crowd are dulled by the water and my splashing. My head grows foggy and all I can think of now is my sister, the young girl, and the old lady who are going through the same experience as me. Accepting my fate, my flailing arms begin to slow. The noise outside the barrel lessens until there is only silence. In this moment I feel I can hear my own thoughts.

Then I hear a voice: "Zerina." I can't help but feel that madness has taken hold of me.

"Zerina, can you hear me?" The words are as clear as glass, and cut me just as deep. I haven't heard Lyrissa's unbroken voice since before her addiction to magic engulfed her. I hear her words as if we are standing beside each other, despite my head being under water. I try to pull my head up from the barrel, but a hand grips me in place.

"We don't have long." Her soft voice continues as if serenading me through the darkness. "Clear your mind. I will be able to hear your thoughts."

*I'm scared, Lyrissa.* Have I completely lost my mind? Has the lack of air brought me to this point?

"Don't be, sister. It is they who should fear you. You have magic within you, too."

I know Lyrissa's words are true. We all have magic, but out of the three of us, my connection is the weakest. After seeing Lyrissa succumb to the addiction, I vowed never to use it again, never to allow myself to be trapped in my own body, a prisoner of the mind.

"You have two options, Zerina. Either accept this fate and slip away into death." I have missed her voice so much. "Or you use your magic, and you fight."

*But they will kill me if they see me use magic*, I argue within my own thoughts.

"Then fight!" she orders. "Zerina?"

Yes, sister?

"Thank you." It is strange to hear her voice but her words have calmed me to a point where I no longer struggle.

The hand forcing my head down grabs hold of my hair

and rips me out of the water. This time I do not panic. I take in a long, deep breath of crisp air. Surveying my surroundings, I see three other barrels nearby. I am saddened at the sight of the older lady, who lies sodden and limp on the ground, her body lifeless.

There is frantic splashing in between the chorus of boos that taunt us as we receive our punishment. The young girl is brought up from the water. She gulps for air. Her cries for them to stop go unheard, and she is forced back under just as the hand that grips me begins to press me forward once more. I am too weak to fight back, but as the water draws close, I see the other barrel. This one has Lyrissa submerged. There is no one holding her down and her body hangs freely from the wooden tomb she lies in. My sister is dead.

My face slaps the water, the cold chill stinging my cheeks. I let out a scream of anguish with the realisation that Lyrissa has been drowned. First Briasse, now her. When will this infernal suffering end?

Lyrissa used her last moments to communicate with me.

My scream turns into a roar, forcing bubbles from my mouth. How dare they, how dare these people treat us this way. They slaughter us like feral animals.

My veins begin to burn. It is a dull feeling at first, but within moments my arms feel as though they are on fire. The pain is immense, and it takes my mind away from the constant battle for air. I open my hands as wide as I can, feeling as if my palms are about to explode. The pressure is unbearable.

The magic escapes my hands unexpectedly. The barrel explodes, and splinters of wood catapult through the air like needles, spraying those in proximity. People wail as

23

wood embeds into their skin. I have no sympathy; it is the least they deserve for their abject cruelty.

The water from my barrel cascades around me.

"Witch!" a voice growls from behind me. The guard's grip loosens from my head as he reaches for his sword.

My arms burn, glowing like molten rock. It is agonising. I take hold of the guard's arms and squeeze.

His face drains of all colour, and he screams in agony as my hands burn through his flesh. He begins to shake uncontrollably from the pain. I enjoy every moment.

I let him go and he drops to the ground. Previously entertained, now the crowd is running away, fearful for their safety, and rightfully so.

My eyes also burn. I am unable to tell if this is from tears or magic as I make my way towards the girl who continues to be held under water.

I have never wielded magic in this manner, and I am afraid it will engulf me. But as much as it hurts, it gives me a feeling of power and exhilaration. A group of guards move towards me, and I instinctively raise my hand before brushing it through the air as if painting a canvas. A blast of flames consumes the three guards, who run screaming as their lives draw to an end. Whatever pain they are feeling pales in comparison to my own.

If I can just save the girl, then I can figure out a way to get out of here, get us to safety somewhere.

My hand is glowing white. Reaching the girl's barrel, I press my palm into the back of the guard's head. He drops, letting go of the girl, who pulls herself up for air as soon as she feels the pressure reduced.

The girl looks at me in shock, dazed by what is happening. Guards are shouting and calling all around, while the people of this poisonous city scatter in every direction, like rats looking for safety. I can only imagine the demon that the girl sees in front of her. In the water, I glimpse my glowing red eyes, as if replaced by flames, and it shocks me.

I feel a greater sense of control and the pain in my arms begins to subside as the magic runs its course.

"Come on, we need to move," I tell the girl. I place my hand out for her to hold. She hesitates, then takes it, and I lead her away.

I have no idea which way to go. There are people running in every direction, away from us. I see a side street and make my way towards it, following a small crowd of evacuees. I am surprised that there are not more sentries descending on us, but as we make our way, I see a man engaged in combat with the guards. His long brown hair is loose and held into place with a black bandana. He looks reasonably dressed and I wonder what quarrel he has with the guards. An executioner lies bloodied and lifeless, and three others are injured. Whatever his fight is, the man is certainly good with his blade.

"This way." I pull the girl with me, who does not seem fully aware of the chaos around us.

"Get them!" someone yells from behind us.

I recognise the voice: it is that of the man who led my capture.

Running in sodden dresses proves difficult, hindering our escape. My dress catches under my feet, and I stumble before tripping over and sliding through the mud.

"Kill them! Don't let them escape!"

I roll onto my back and see that the a guard has hold of the girl. He smiles at me as he draws a dagger from his side. I do not know who he is going to strike first.

"Please don't – " I barely speak my words before the man's blood sprays across my face. A sword protrudes from

25

his neck. His eyes fade as he slips away. When he falls, our rescuer stands behind him. The man with the bandana.

His dark eyes and stubbled face are more endearing than I expected for someone who has just taken a life. A scar crosses his right cheek. With a calmness that I do not feel, he offers his hand to help me to my feet.

Then he turns his attentions to the girl. "Esara!" he exclaims, dropping his sword where he stands.

Her eyes light up and a smile engulfs her face in pure joy.

"Ulrik!" She wraps her arms and embraces him tightly.

"Come, we need to escape." He holsters his sword and lifts Esara into his arms, then turns to me. "Are you coming?"

As we make off down the street, I pray that this man knows what he is doing.

# 6

## ULRIK

I have her. After all these years, I am reunited with Esara. She is shaken to the core from what she has witnessed today. No child should ever be exposed to this. Our mother has been taken from us and we will grieve for her, but right now my focus is on getting my sister to safety.

The magic I witnessed is as mystifying as it is devastating, I have never seen it before, and would not like to face such unnatural powers in battle. The woman who wields it looks timid now, a far cry from just a short while ago when her arms burned brightly with fire. Now she sits behind me as we make our way over the Biterian Plains on my horse, her hands wrapped tightly around me. Esara sits in front of me, her hair flowing behind her as she embraces the breeze that greets us. I am grateful that I purchased a sizeable horse on my return from the *Iris*. He has earned himself as many apples as he so desires.

"We need to stop for a short while," I say. "The horse needs a rest if we are to continue to Uster." I see a small cluster of trees which will offer us some shield, should the guards come after us, though we were not followed out of Eltera's gates. I can only assume this is because of their fear of Zerina's magic, or the fires needed extinguishing.

"Have you not named him?" Esara's sweet voice asks.

"I've been a little busy, sister."

Esara leans forward as we begin to slow, and strokes the steed's white mane.

I bring us to a stop and the woman behind me slides off the back. She has remained silent for the past few hours, and does not look ready for conversation. Her face is saddened, her jet-black hair matted, her skin covered in dirt. Her eyes draw me in. They are as blue as the ocean, and even in her current state there is still a spark within them.

I lift Esara down and smile at her. Despite what she has been through, she is still able to muster a smile back. We hug tightly and I place my hand on her head.

"I love you," I tell her. "As long as I am around, I will always keep you safe, I promise you this."

Esara pulls away and launches herself at the woman, her guardian. I owe Esara's life to her, and words alone cannot do justice to my gratitude. I do not care if she bears magic; she showed compassion for my sister in her time of need. Esara wraps herself around the woman and I see her stormy eyes soften. She hugs her back as if the two are comforting one another.

"Thank you," says Esara.

"I am so sorry for your mother, I wish I could have saved her."

"Did you lose anyone?" Esara asks as she looks up into the woman's eyes.

The woman's gaze become vacant and she stares through me as if I am not there. "My sisters. I lost my sisters, little one."

28

Tears begin to fill Esara's eyes, and she hugs the woman again. Despite her own grief, she shows nothing but empathy for the woman's feelings, and I feel pride at the young woman she is becoming.

"Does my sister's saviour have a name?" I ask.

She stifles back her tears before stammering on her words. "My name is Zerina." She doesn't look at me when she speaks.

"Thank you," I start. "Thank you for saving Esara." These are the only words I can manage as my thoughts drift to my murdered mother. "I dread to think of Esara's fate should you not have intervened."

"She is just a girl. It is wrong what they have done."

Esara breaks away and runs into my embrace. I tighten my arms around her and we cry together. I try to hold back the tears, but I am unable to. I have waited so long to see my family, and now my mother is gone and my sister orphaned.

"I know your sister's name, but please tell me yours so I may address you."

"Apologies, Zerina, my name is Ulrik. I don't mean to be rude. It's just I haven't seen my sister in so long." I nod my head to her. I would have tipped my hat towards her but I lost it in the fight.

"Pleased to meet your acquaintance, Ulrik." Zerina curtsies which I do not expect. "Thank you for saving me."

"It would seem that we owe thanks to one another." I smile, then I notice that Esara and Zerina both draw cold breaths and are beginning to shiver. Their clothes are still wet. "There is a tavern not far from here. Once our horse is rested, we will make our way there."

"What if the guards stop there in search of us?" Esara asks. "What if they catch us and do all that to us again?"

Being submerged under water would be a kindness compared to what they would have in store for us if they were to catch us. "There are many a tavern across the plains, too many for the Elterian guards to search all of them."

It's not the best plan, but at the moment, it is all I have.

# 7
## ZERINA

*'Yakula fur is a sought after material. It's magical properties enabling the wearer to remain warm in the coldest of conditions.'*
*Armour Index - Kings Guard 257 KR*

The fire cracks and the embers float into the chimney. I rub my hands together, trying to warm up in the cosy room we now find ourselves in. It is a coldness like I have never felt, it chills me to my bones. Esara is clean and dry, and now lies asleep in the bed at the other side of the room, wrapped in a sheepskin quilt. Ulrik had to settle her for some time before she fell asleep. The poor girl is exhausted from the day and for a short period at least should find peace whilst dreaming.

Ulrik sits by the window keeping watch on the street below for any signs of the Elterian guards. His face is stony as he concentrates, the scar on his cheek looking more pronounced in this light.

I have been unable to warm myself since we arrived, no

matter how hard I try. A hot bath did not help. It is as though I have been walking through deep snow after going for a swim in an icy lake. My teeth chitter uncontrollably, and the temptation to jump into the fire crosses my mind on more than one occasion.

"Why is it you do not warm?" Ulrik steers his eyes away from the window momentarily. "Are you sick?"

"It's – it's the magic that I used in Eltera," I stammer, struggling to form my sentences. "I saw my sister go through this so many times. Each time she used her magic her body would be affected in different ways. Shivers, boils, aged skin, high fevers. She experienced all of it."

"How long does it last for?" Ulrik asks. He looks concerned at my fragile state.

"Until we use our magic again. It is a curse. The more magic we use, the worse the side effects. As you can see, I used a lot of magic in Eltera, and now I am paying the consequences." I picture Lyrissa, and shudder, nearly forgetting, for a moment, that she is gone now.

"I watched my sister succumb to this affliction," I continue. "I watched as her body decayed as she lived. Her teeth cracked, and her skin aged beyond her years. If I was to use some magic it may help my symptoms but then my body would bear further consequence. The greater the use, the greater the burden."

"Is there anything that can be done to ease it?"

"I have to ride through these side effects. This magic will make my body do strange things, all with the aim of getting me to harness the magic in my blood again. It is a curse I would not wish on anyone." I shuffle closer to the fire, unable to feel any warmth that it produces.

"Careful, you may burn your skin," Ulrik warns me.

I move back again. There is nothing I can do other than

wait for these symptoms to subside. A pain flows down both my arms as if ice has replaced my bones. It is a pain that I cannot isolate, and it becomes too much for me. I cry out in pain, and tears run down my cheek, dropping onto the dust-covered floorboards. I try to internalise my pain as best as I can, not wanting to wake Esara who is blissfully unaware of my plight. I wish to keep it this way, and I try to bring my screams of pain under control.

I hadn't noticed Ulrik get up, but now the rough fibres of a blanket slide over me. I take hold of both sides and wrap it as tightly as I can around me. I appreciate the sentiment, but I do not believe it will help. The chill I feel is not physical.

"I do not see it as a curse," Ulrik says as he removes a pot from the fire and pours liquid into a cup. He passes it to me. "If not for your actions, my sister would be dead. What you have is a gift, and gifts need cherishing." There is a softness to his voice, and I find that he gives good counsel.

But it doesn't reduce my pain, and the tremor in my hand almost causes me to spill the contents of the hot brew all over myself. Ulrik kneels in front of me and places his hands on either side of my own to help steady them. I can feel the roughness of his palms against my skin, and for a brief moment I feel the faintest of warmth as the contents of the cup act as a conduit.

My tremor steadies and he helps me bring the stew to my lips. I feel the contents run down my throat and the hot mixture brings me some comfort. I quickly take another sip when I realise that the stew soothes my coldness.

"Careful, you'll cause yourself a greater injury drinking at that speed." Ulrik prompts me to lower my hands, then returns to the window.

"D-d-did you know?" I ask, still shivering.

Ulrik doesn't appear to understand the nature of my question.

"That your mother carried magic?" I clarify.

Ulrik looks away from me and out the window, as if staring to the skies for guidance. "I do not wish to discuss it," he says sharply, and I am taken aback by the coldness in his voice. "You need to try and rest. We will ride to Uster as soon as light breaks." He positions himself so that his body no longer faces my direction, and I worry that I have offended him in some way.

"Why Uster?"

"We are now wanted criminals. If we can find a boat, the sea will offer us refuge. Get some sleep. I will keep watch." There is a sternness to his voice and I feel this is not a request he is making and more a command.

"You need sleep, too."

"I will sleep when it is safe to do so." He turns back to the window, and I know the conversation is over.

Deep down, I believe that Ulrik will remain true to his word, but I wonder how long it will be until we are safe.

# 8

## ULRIK

As we reach Uster the next morning, Esara sits side-on, cuddling into me as we ride. The ground is softening as dirt is replaced with sand, the breeze picking up as we approach the port. Behind me, Zerina holds onto me more loosely than she did yesterday. She has hardly spoken a word, and I know I am to blame for this. I spoke to her out of turn last night when she asked me if I knew about my mother, but the memories are too painful, too raw.

The truth is, I have always known of my mother's abilities. Esara has never displayed any affinity for magic, but just in case, our mother always fed Esara a potion to suppress any powers she might have. As long as she drinks this potion, her magic will stay hidden, and even she need not know she possesses it.

I will apologise to Zerina when I get the chance. For now, I must focus on getting the ingredients I need to brew the potion for Esara. It has been years, but the recipe is seared into my mind from helping my mother brew it many times.

We reach the outskirts of Uster and I shuffle Esara forward before climbing down from Sovren, which is the name Esara has bestowed upon my horse. Being one of the smaller ports in Levanthria, it has been some time since I last laid eyes on this town, famed for the fishing trade it centres around. There is no pomposity here; this is a town full to the brim of men and women seeking to earn a living. Given the hardships that are befalling the people across Levanthria through taxation, it is refreshing to see such an honest place still thriving.

"What are you doing, Ulrik?" Esara appears somewhat bemused by my sudden dismount, her eyebrows lowering as she addresses me.

"Eltera will have sent word. There will be people looking for us," I tell her as I remove my satchel from Sovren's saddle. "I need you two to ride Sovren down this road here. It should be quiet, and it will lead you to the docks."

"You're leaving us?" Zerina spits, speaking to me for the first time today. She shuffles forward on Sovren and takes his reins.

"Not for long, and only out of necessity," I assure her, but she scowls at me with disapproval. I do not like the idea any more than she does. "I need to collect some items from the market. The three of us riding through will draw too much attention. Especially if word has already reached here about your escape. I will meet you by the docks. I have gold coin I plan to barter for safe passage aboard a ship."

"What if we are spotted, brother? How will we keep safe?" Esara attempts to squirm out of the saddle in protest, but I reach forward and steady her.

"You are safe with Zerina. You have seen what she can do."

"I want to go home."

I gently place my hand on Esara's cheek. "We cannot stay here, nor can we return once we have left. Our life here will soon be a distant memory."

Esara's eyes well up and she looks away. I wipe away one of her tears with my thumb before smacking the rear of Sovren, encouraging him to set off. "I will see you by the docks. I won't be long. If you are spotted, run," I call out as Zerina takes control of the horse and they ride away.

I head in the opposite direction, towards the markets. I am soon within the confines of the streets, hidden in the crowds of people who go about their daily trades. The smell of fish greets me, causing a pang of hunger to growl from my stomach. I purchase a few apples from a fruit stand, including extras for Sovren. The sharp, crisp taste causes a refreshing sourness in my cheeks, and will hopefully settle my hunger.

Next, I find an elderly lady who grasps a bunch of dried leaves in her hands. She wears a blue cloak and looks as if she lives in the wild. As I approach, the incense of burning sage greets me. The woman picks it up and shakes it around her, as seers do, to cleanse the air around them.

"May I trouble you for some herbs, miss?" I politely ask, bending closer to speak in a hushed tone. You never know who might be listening. "I am looking for some vipe seeds, snapwire leaves, dried terilion, and quaro powder."

I feel the woman's gaze burrow deep within me.

"I do not mean to cause offence, but I would appreciate it if you did not use you seer abilities on me. I make my own fate." One must be firm with seers. If allowed, they will soon have you buying more items to change a fate they profess to have seen, and these fates are always dire.

The woman snaps back, and her eyes becr

vacant as the colour returns to them. "Apologies," she replies with a crackling voice, and I wonder if it's from inhaling too much incense in her life. "It's just, you have an interesting future, like none I have ever seen."

I school my expression to hide my impatience. "Do you have the items that I request?"

Finally, she begins collecting jars and vials, but she takes her time. I scan my surroundings in frustration. The longer I am here, the greater the chance of me being spotted by the guards.

The seer is unsteady on her feet and uses a small cane to keep her balance. Her legs look ready to break as she moves, such is the delicate frame that she carries. "As interesting as your fate is, I am more drawn to that of your sister." Her wrinkled hand reaches for a small jar which I recognise as quaro powder.

"My sister?" I, of course, did not tell her about Esara.

The seer wraps the jars in fabric to form a parcel, her hands moving slowly. "I see ships, treasures, and a fury as wild as the sea you seek to set sail on." She passes me my items and I give the old woman some coin, plus a little extra for her foresight.

The temptation is too great. "Will she be safe? Will she live to a good age?" I press. I need to leave, quickly, but not before I seek assurance about Esara's safety.

"She looks like you. She is not safe, but she is able to live a good life from what she has learned from you."

Esara resembles our mother, not me. Maybe the woman has taken a lucky guess that I have a sister, and the reference to setting sail would apply to many travellers in Uster. It is, after all, a port town.

"Thank you, for your goods and for the foresight." I tuck the parcel under my arm and walk away.

One thing I am sure of is that my plan to board a boat is the right one. I can agree with the seer that our future now lies out at sea.

# 9

## ZERINA

'*On the seventeenth day in the 17th month of the Great War King Athos did something that changed the landscape of Levanthria forever. He agreed to the use of magic in his desperation to to turn the tides of war in his favour.*'

*Volume VXII of The History of Levanthria - 260 KR*

The water by the harbour is calm and lies flat. I've heard that all manner of creatures make this fascinating expanse of ocean their home. It is one of the many stories that Bri told me when we were younger. She was lucky enough to see the sea before, but I never have, until now.

The beautiful, glistening blue is far bigger than I could have ever imagined. There are men and women spread out along the shore with long sticks that have threads hanging from the end which are dipped into the water. As we walk by them, I see a bucket that has some small-finned creatures which I assume are fish. I couldn't be certain, as I have never seen one before. Taking a closer look, I can see two large teeth protruding from the orange and green creature, its green, bulging eyes still flicking around as it takes its last breaths. There is a strong smell in the air which is not particularly pleasant but once we pass where people fish this seems to fade.

Ahead there is a wooden platform that sits atop the water. It looks like it has seen better days. The ramshackle planks of wood look as if a strong wind would see it disintegrate, but the number of people walking up and down it would tell me that it is sturdier than it looks.

Four vessels sit on the water that vary in size, all bound with thick rope to the side of the docks. One is small and two are bigger, but the fourth dwarfs the others in size. Cannons peep out of holes in the side of its hull.

I can hear the voices of the men and women on board as they get ready to set sail. A deathly thin man unties the rope that attaches the ship to the dock, then calls up once he is done. A woman who sits at the top of the mast relays the message. The ship creaks as it begins to slowly move away from the harbour wall.

I smile at the spectacle. "I've never seen a ship before," I tell Esara. I feel like a small insect in comparison.

"Really?" Esara exclaims, her hands stroking Sovren's mane. "How can you reach your age and never have seen a boat?"

A tut leaves my mouth. "I would not consider twenty an old age," I muse. "My sisters and I have always lived in the hills of Pendara. I was always told it was too unsafe to visit anywhere else, so I have spent most of my life up there."

"That must have been boring," Esara replies, but her face falls. The sweet child is probably unable to comprehend the risk only until yesterday, and I am sure she thinks of her mother.

Living in Pendara is a life that I was used to and one that I would go back to in a heartbeat, even if it was boring.

My fascination with the boat setting sail almost causes me to steer Sovren into a tubby man who carries a basket of fish. His bald head drips with sweat, and his clothes are wet from wrestling with the fish.

"Sorry sir, I —"

"Watch where you're going, you migwall!" he roars, his face reddening as he loses his balance.

"Who are you calling migwall, you bloated yarwool!" Esara snipes back.

He loses his grip on the basket and it skims to the floor, the fish sliding back into the sea.

His cheeks puff out profusely at his displeasure. "Reckon you owe me a few coins for that, girls." He grabs the horse's harness. "You're not going anywhere until you have given me what is owed." His voice is like gravel, and the way he looks at us makes me feel uneasy.

"I am sorry, sir, but we have no coin to offer you."

A wide grin engulfs his face, revealing his yellow-stained teeth. "There is another way in which I can receive payment." His eyes look over me, and I shudder at the thoughts that ravage his mind as he undresses me with his eyes. I feel sick to my stomach when he then does the same with Esara.

"Sir, I advise you to avert your dark thoughts. Please leave my sister and me alone." In the moment, calling her sister is the only reason I can muster for the two of us to be travelling together.

"Sister?" the slimy man scoffs. "There's nothing sisterly about you two. Tell me, what business do you have in Uster?"

"That's none of your concern," Esara spits. She tries to kick the man away from us but her legs are too short.

His yellow smile widens. "Got some spunk about her, hasn't she? I will accept her as payment. Or maybe I should just inform those guards over there of our quarrel." He offers his hand out to Esara. "If you would be so kind."

I feel like I am going to be sick. We have already caused enough of a scene, and the last thing we need is to draw the guards' attention.

"I will return payment," I tell him, lowering myself down from the horse.

"No, Zerina," Esara protests, but I see what little choice we have in this situation.

"Stay here, sister."

The man offers his hand to me, unable to hide his delight. I ignore him and begin what I imagine to be a confident walk to the alleyway on the other side of the street. In truth, I have no idea what to do. I have never been with a man, and never imagined it would happen like this.

"Do not move from that spot." I look Esara dead in the eye. Her eyes are wet, but I know she will listen to me. I cannot let her endure this bulbous cyst of a man. The best I can do is give the appearance of confidence and control, even if inside I am trembling and terrified of what awaits me once we are alone.

The alley is small and compact, and the uneasy ground is caked with mud. The walls of the buildings on either side are cracked and crumbling. Vermin scurry for whatever food they can find in small clusters, scavenging to survive. I can relate to the desperation they must feel just to stay alive.

The shadows linger ahead, and the man steps into the alley, blocking out the light. I barely have time to think before he is upon me, pressing me to the wall, his strength far greater than my own. Panic overcomes me, and I struggle to free my arms but he possesses a vice-like grip.

He brings his face closer to me. His skin is oily and cracked where pox infection has left crater-sized holes in his face. The repugnant fragrance of fish clings to him, and his odious presence nearly forces me to wretch. As he presses against me I move my head to the side, not wanting to see his face. All I can do is accept what is about to happen.

Or you use your magic, and you fight.

Lyrissa would fight. Bri would fight.

A spark ignites within me. How dare this man demand use of my body. How dare the people of this kingdom execute and torture us for having magic.

An anger rises within me, and my arms begin to burn. Tears settle in my eyes, not from the pain, but from the injustice.

"Stop," I tell the man.

"I'll stop when I have received my payment." His breath is close enough for me to feel it against my skin. It makes me feel dirty, the smell of him is unbearable.

"Don't – "

He presses himself against me. As my fear and anger rise, so does the temperature in my arms. The smell of fish is replaced by burning flesh as his hands crack and sizzle.

He loosens his grip. His screams of pain echo through the alley, and I place both my hands against his chest and push him away from me. They glow white as stars as they burn through his clothes, branding his chest to the shape of my open palms.

I can't help but smile at his squeals of pain. It is the least he deserves. I feel powerful and in control. My heart

44

races as the magic courses through my veins, and I am utterly alive as I press my hands harder against his chest.

The man's eyes go wide and vacant, and he crumples to the floor, whimpering like a babe. The smoke from his singed flesh rises above him as I make my way back to Esara.

To my freedom.

# IO
## ULRIK

I hear echoed screams, and I fear the worst. It draws the attention of the guards and I make haste to reach the docks before they do.

Esara sits on top of Sovren by the harbour. My gaze quickly diverts to Zerina, who is leaving an alleyway in a hasty manner, peering back over her shoulder.

The guards are beginning to rally. Esara cries uncontrollably on Sovren, drawing further unwelcome attention to us.

"What is it? What happened?" I ask.

Esara struggles to form her words. "It's Zerina! We nearly trampled a man, and he lost his stock. He demanded payment." Her eyes light up when she sees Zerina crossing the road towards us.

Zerina's face is paler than usual, and her dress is ruffled. She continues to survey her surroundings, breaking out into jog.

"What's going on here?" a guard asks her briskly.

Zerina ignores the guard, which is not the wisest move, and she continues in our direction.

The guard peers into the side street before turning to face us. "Stop them!" he cries, "She's a witch! She has attacked a man!" His voice echoes in the open streets and the rest of the guards' attention switches to us in an instant.

"So much for keeping out of trouble," I mutter as I jump onto Sovren's back and take the reins from Esara. I gee him on and we move to Zerina. I offer her my hand, which she accepts, and I pull her up to ride behind me.

The guards call out their commands, waving wildly in our direction.

"I leave you for not thirty minutes," I say as we set of towards the harbour platform. There is nowhere else to go.

"He deserved it," Zerina calls over the sound of Sovren's hooves. "He wanted your sister, not me." She tucks her head into my back and wraps her arms tightly around my waist.

Our advantage is that the guards are on foot, which means we can make good ground, but we are fast running out of it. We reach the pier and Sovren bucks. I do not blame him; the weathered dock does not look steady for a horse.

Ahead of us sits a ship that has seen better days. I assume it has made harbour for repairs, but as far as I can see, it is unmanned. The hull is splintered, and large broken planks are snapped. Parts are missing where they should be; a sure sign that it has been besieged by pirates while on its voyage. The sails hang loosely, the white fabric catching the wind.

We have no other option. I urge the steed along the pier.

"Where do you take us?" Zerina asks, her grip tightening.

The guards are making ground and we need to act

quickly. I encourage the horse to move a little faster, and he thankfully obliges.

"We are taking that ship."

"Taking a ship? How exciting!" Esara exclaims, as if this is all a game. I am grateful in this moment that she is not as fearful as most children are at her age.

"How? There are only three of us," Zerina says.

I want to tell her that we will all hang for our crimes when the guards catch us. Instead I say, "It's not that big, you could probably get away with ten men to man it." My calculations are optimistic at best. I don't tell her that, either.

"But there are *three* of us!"

"But two of you are witches."

Esara spins her head around at my words, but I don't have time to explain to her.

I bring Sovren to a halt and urge the others to dismount. "Go," I command, and they don't argue. Zerina and Esara scramble from Sovren's back and make their way along the platform that connects the pier to the ship.

I gallop down the pier towards the front of the ship, where I pull out my sword and take a wild swing at the rope that anchors it in place. The rope doesn't cut. We're running out of time.

I turn and take another swing with my sword, and the rope detaches. All that remains is the rope at the rear of the boat. I race back, but by now the guards have drawn close. There are at least two dozen of them, and their calls for our capture ring loud. I dismount and swing at the rope with all the strength that I can muster.

"Stop!"

"Turn yourself in!"

"Get away from that ship!"

I hack at the rope wildly, attempting to break us free from the land.

"Come on!" I shout in frustration. The rope snaps, and the wood from the ship groans as it breathes into life.

The guards are upon me. I point my blade towards them as I walk backwards up the platform. I have no intention of turning myself in.

A guard rushes at me and attempts to strike me with his blade. I quickly parry this to my right, then strike him with my free hand. Another man jabs at me but I step back and stomp on the sword before kicking the soldier into the water.

More guards rally at the pier as I reach the top of the platform where Zerina and Esara wait, and three more begin to run towards us. I grab hold of the platform and lift with all my might. It has the weight of the men on it, but the ship groaning away from the pier aids me, and I move it just enough to break the connection. The plank grinds against the edge of the ship before dropping into the sea, followed by the splashing of the guards who cry out for help.

"Esara, get ready to steer."

She nods.

I run to the mast and throw my weight into it to dislodge it. I am not strong enough on my own.

"Zerina!" I yell. It won't take the guards long to recover, and we are not safe yet.

Not needing an explanation, she rushes to my side and the two of us push with everything we have. To my relief, it begins to move. As the gods look down on us, the wind takes hold of the sails at the perfect moment, and we edge away from the pier.

The guards scream profanities at us, but their shouts are in vain.

The ship's pace picks up as we make our escape.

We have done it. We have a ship and with it we can sail to our freedom.

# II

## ZERINA

'*Fairy dust is believed to carry magical properties. It is because of this that they are sought after on the black market. The dust is made from a fairy's burnt embers, or so they say.*'

*Magic and Monsters - 247 KR*

My head throbs to its core, another side effect from using my newfound abilities. I sit in the captain's quarters, which are in worse condition than my house in Pendara. The smell of damp, rotting wood welcomes me to my new abode.

The sea feels calm as we set off out into the big wide ocean, but Ulrik has informed me that this will not always be the case. The waters may be calm now, but that does not stop the ship from swaying back and forth to our unknown destination. The boat creaks and groans as it fights against the waves beneath us. Surely the ship will sink at the first opportunity.

I search through the drawers of a ramshackle desk,

exhaling in frustration when I find them empty. There is another loud creak, followed by a slight bump, and I my anxieties spike. Specks of light pierce the gaps above me like the sun's rays shining through heavy clouds. I am grateful that the weather treats us with some kindness, and to our surprise, no ships have given chase. Given my luck of late, I am more than happy for the reprieve.

There is a delicate knock at the door, followed by Esara a few seconds later. Her hair is wild and wind-whipped, and a rare smile decorates her angelic face. "This is so exciting, isn't it?" Her face beams with innocence and joy, a far cry from the torment I am feeling in this moment.

"Ulrik has had a look around the ship," she tells me. "He says there are problems with part of the mast, and the cargo hold. Also the rudder system, which is making the ship drag." She does not seem the least bit perturbed by what sounds like bad news. "He doesn't think they will follow us, because the ship is in such a state of disrepair."

I hear her words, but my mind is elsewhere, to the memory of my hands burning through the man's flesh until I felt his bone. I have never inflicted so much pain onto another. True, he was about to do the unthinkable to me, but it scares me to think I am capable of subjecting a person to such agony. All the hurt and pain I have endured got the better of me when I released my power.

My hands throb with pain from the magic I used. In that moment, I felt alive, energised. Now, in the aftermath of my actions, I feel empty and in pain. When I run my fingers through my hair, it feels like barbed wire.

"What's wrong?"

"I just have a headache." I do not wish to burden Esara with my troubles.

Esara looks saddened by this but then her frown is

quickly replaced by an energetic smile. "Come with me." She gestures for me to follow, exiting the captain's quarters and heading out to the main deck.

I reluctantly follow her, wishing to stay inside where it is darker, where I can rest. As I step outside, the sunlight makes my eyes sting, and fresh sea air prickles my skin. I fight the temptation to return to the captain's quarters and hide.

"Come here, come see." Esara races up the main deck to the top of the ship.

"Esara, be careful, I do not wish to see you fall in from the side!" Ulrik's words come from somewhere above me, and I search for his position. He stands on higher level, hands on the wheel.

"I will be fine! Zerina, come with me."

I cast Ulrik a nervous smile and follow Esara across the main deck. We are not moving at speed but I am conscious of the boat as it rocks, nearly knocking me off balance.

"You will get used to it," Ulrik reassures me with a smile on his face.

Esara peers out over the front of the ship, her untamed blond hair blowing behind her. "Look at it, it's beautiful isn't it?" Her eyes are wide as she takes in the open view of the ocean.

Serene waters lie ahead, birds fly high above, and a clear blue sky embraces us. In this moment, I can see why someone would wish to live the life of a sailor.

"It is certainly beautiful," I reply, feeling reassured by the peaceful waters.

"Ulrik was away on a ship for seven years. I missed him every day that he was gone. But when you see this view, it makes more sense." She takes a large intake of air and savours it.

I close my eyes and let my senses guide me, letting the cold air press against me. The pain in my arms slowly subsides. The warmth of the sun beams down on my face as I relax to the sound of the ship pushing through the water. The weight of what has happened to my sisters passes over me, and it suffocates me. Tears stream down my face and my chest heaves, then grief consumes me.

Esara seems to panic at my reaction and casts a look to her brother. She rushes into me and offers me a hug. I embrace her, wondering how is it that a child can be so brave under such adversity while I crumble like ruined castle walls.

I sob, finding it hard to draw breath as my thoughts finally react to the fate that has befallen Bri and Lyrissa, how their lives have been snatched from them. It isn't fair. My sisters are gone and I am alone in the world. When Esara releases me, I turn to make my leave, not wishing for her to see me like this.

My heart jolts as I lose my footing and panic consumes me. My ankle has caught on some loose rope, and I stumble into the railing.

"Zerina!" Esara cries.

Her shouts become distant, as a weighted feeling engulfs my stomach. I tumble over the side of the ship towards the water below. Time feels as though it stops on my descent, and a memory flashes across my mind: the comfort of being at home with my sisters. Sitting in front of a smouldering fire whilst feeding Lyrissa in between her madness-induced words. I can smell the peat burning on the fire, taste the sweetness of the porridge oats, hear Briasse's humming as she looks out the window over the hills.

A searing pain flashes into the forefront of my mind and

the image is replaced by the angered crowd calling for our heads, accusing us of being witches. I panic as if I am back there, in the very moment we were captured. All the fear, the anger, the hatred rushes back to me.

The water pulls me in and consumes me, the coldness like nothing I have ever felt. I have had my fair share of cold nights living in the Pendaran Hills, but those pale in comparison to what I feel now. Ice-cold water wraps around me like a frigid blanket, and there is nothing I can do other than embrace it. My breath is taken in an instant and I feel as though my lungs will implode as I franticly struggle to the surface. My arms and legs flail but my dress makes it impossible for me to swim. As hard as I try, my legs tangle in the trail of the fabric, and the weight of it pulls me deeper into the darkening abyss. I wave my arms in front of me, clawing through the water in desperation. The light from above seems farther and farther away. I realise I am sinking to my grave.

An agonising pain flashes inside my head and it's enough to make the coldness that engulfs me a distant thought.

I stand over a table, looking down at piece of parchment. It is a map. To the left, a point marks *Uster* on the landmass that is labelled *Levanthria.* Further landmasses are scattered across the map, some small, some large with pictures of mountains, trees, and temples that look like they were etched onto the parchment by the owner of the map. I never realised how small Levanthria was, and suddenly the world feels a whole lot bigger.

An island to the south is circled but I am unable to make out the words underneath. They appear to be written in Elvish. I recognise the letters from an old book of Bri's.

"Voraz."

The image of the map vanishes from my mind as the clearly spoken word reaches me. I open my eyes and see nothing but darkness around me, the muffled distorted sounds of the ocean as I drown.

"You must travel to Voraz."

Lyrissa. It is as clear as if she floats in the water alongside me.

The map springs into my mind again, this time closer to the circled island. Flashes of a prosperous land, flashes of luxuries and unspeakable treasures. I see an opening to a cave, a man chanting an Elvish incantation. Vines begin to grow around the entrance, concealing it. The mage turns and looks me dead in the eyes. A searing, pressurised pain threatens to cause my head to implode. He appears to share my pain, and he stumbles, his hand leaving an imprint in the stone.

"You must find it," comes Lyrissa's sweet, calming voice. "It will help you control it. It will take away the pain." Her voice soothes me, but it brings me pain to know I will never see her again.

Am I in the afterlife? Is this why I hear my sister speak so clearly?

"Voraz, Zerina, you must travel to Voraz, find the cave."

Water boils around me, and my heart is ready to burst from my chest. A heat rises inside me and I realise it is my magic that causes the current. The exhilaration warms my every part. As I push up through the water, the light from above grows in intensity. I keep going until I feel the warmth of the sun on my face.

I gasp for air, flailing my arms as I try not to sink once more.

"Zerina!" Ulrik calls. Something splashes toward me,

but I am too burdened by my dress to answer. My legs are too heavy.

"I've got you," Ulrik says. He wraps his muscular arm around me, and I pull my hand up to hold onto his forearm. "Don't worry I've got you."

"Voraz," I sputter. "We must sail to Voraz."

# 12

## ULRIK

"Voraz." I speak the name of the island Zerina muttered as I dragged her from the water. I stand at the ship's wheel, still sodden from jumping in after her, but slowly drying with the fresh breeze. The ocean has already reminded me of how dangerous it can be. It is a miracle that Zerina did not lose her life and sink to the depths of the dark abyss below.

I did not think that so little time would pass before I found myself back at sea. The ship sails steady, much to my surprise. Even though the water is relatively settled, the ship rocks back and forth, something that I find soothes my mind like an infant being cradled by a parent.

But ahead, the waters are blackened and the waves break to reveal white edges. A storm is coming, and I worry the ship isn't up to the task. As much as I feel at ease at sea, and I welcome the distraction from thoughts of my mother, I fear this ship will sink under the right conditions. My old captain would be appalled to see a ship in such disrepair.

Less than a week ago, I was an honoured privateer, given leave from service on the *Iris* as ordered by King

Athhos. Now I find myself tethered to a new ship, a wanted fugitive. All the years of service I dedicated have been undone by my actions, actions I would repeat if the opportunity presented itself again.

I am ashamed of what Levanthria has become in my absence, of the atrocities that are committed to people just for bearing magic. If this is the way our kingdom is to be run, then I want no part in it. The kingdom I served faithfully for seven years is now our enemy. I know that treason is what they will call it, but the only crimes I see are the ones that led to the deaths of innocent people, including the murder of my mother.

Thinking of her brings a pain to my chest and an ache to the back of my throat. What I would give for advice from her now. To hear her soft voice offer some words of reassurance. What I would give to allow she and Esara to be reunited. Esara hides her grief from us well, but I know she is hurting.

For now, we must seek land where we can make trade with the coin I still possess. The coin that was intended to get our jarjoba vineyard going. I was supposed to secure a future for my family.

Now, our only chance of survival is a life of piracy.

Using my compass, I navigate southwest, aiming for Voraz. I do not know why Zerina wants to go there, but it's as good a destination as any.

Come nightfall, I will be able to navigate using the stars to find a true path. For now, this will suffice. I can only hope that we do not cross paths with any naval ships while we stay our course.

Zerina and Esara emerge from inside, Esara's face lit up like the brightest of stars. It is an image that fills me with hope.

"She's awake, Ulrik!" Esara has enough energy to do the work of more than one man on this ship.

"I am glad you are okay, Zerina, you gave us quite the scare." I smile at her, relieved that she seems somewhat fresh-faced, given her ordeal.

She smiles and tips her head towards me. "Thank you, Ulrik. If not for your actions, I fear what would have become of me."

"The ocean can be unforgiving, especially this far out. Esara, you did amazing taking control of the ship whilst I aided Zerina."

Esara beams at my words.

"I need one of you to steer for a moment."

Zerina comes to me at once. Her dark hair blows in the breeze, her eyes concentrated on the steps that lead to the quarterdeck. She stumbles as we rock backwards, then lets out a sweet laugh rather than looking embarrassed.

"Here, take hold of the wheel," I tell her, stepping away.

Zerina looks apprehensive and I do not blame her. It is a daunting task, steering a ship. She tentatively places her hands on the wheel, and I feel a spark between us when I lay both my hands over hers.

"You need to feel the ocean. Don't fight against her too much, as she can be ruthless." I stand behind her for a moment longer, then gently release my hold on her arms, giving her full control.

She gasps as she feels the power of the water, but she takes control of the ship, taking to the task like a natural.

"There's so much power," she murmurs. Her hands are tense, her expression calm.

"It will get easier as you get used to it," I reply. "Hold her steady, I won't be long." Our eyes meet for a moment, and she offers me a real smile.

I reach for my overcoat and start to turn away, but something is nagging at me. "When you surfaced from the water, you said the word 'Voraz'. Tell me, how did you come to learn of such an island?" Why, moments away from greeting the afterlife, was this the word that escaped her lips?

Zerina's body stiffens, and she turns her shoulder towards me.

"It is an island inhabited by people who love the life of the open seas, but are less favourable of the naval ships that patrol the waters. Some call them scoundrels, boatswains, powder monkeys. I've come to know them as – "

"Pirates," Zerina cuts me off, not meeting my eyes. "You know, in Eltera, they forced my head into a barrel of water." Zerina gives me a look of sorrow. "In that panic, one of my sisters brought me comfort, but she has spoken nothing but incoherent ramblings since her addiction to magic consumed her."

Zerina sniffles back tears as she brings her gaze out across the ocean. It seems to me that she searches the clouds as if looking for her fallen sisters. "She told me to fight. I had never used my magic before, not like that. It consumed me, Ulrik. But that feeling of control, of power . . . it was like nothing I have ever experienced. It led me to you and your sister."

Zerina brings her arm across her face to wipe away tears. "When I fell into the sea, my sister spoke to me once more."

"Is it possible to communicate with the departed?" I ask as tenderly as I can, a pang of hope rising inside of me. Could I speak to my mother?

"I don't know, Ulrik." Zerina struggles to gather herself, so I step forward and take hold of the wheel from the side, giving her a nod of reassurance. She ducks under my arms as she lets go to give me back control of the ship.

"Lyrissa gave me a vision. I see it quite clearly, in Voraz. A cave hidden by Elven magic. She wants me to find it. I have to find it."

"Are you sure?" I ask. I struggle to hide the doubt in my voice. I've never put much stock in visions.

"If my sister has sent me a sign, I have to follow it."

I hesitate. If I thought my mother had sent me a sign, I'd want to follow it, too. "I understand, Zerina. We go to Voraz and I will help you find this cave."

Maybe it is the will of the gods that our paths have crossed.

# 13

## ULRIK

'*Don't go too close to the waters edge. The swamp hag known as Jinni green teeth may well drag you under.*'
*Tales of the Bard - 233 KR*

Three days later, the gods continue to favour us with calm waters.

Daylight has broken and the sun casts a stretched reflection across the flattened ocean ahead of us. There is barely a wave as we steadily make our way to our destination: Voraz, renowned for drink, debauchery, and trade. Two of the three I have a desire to engage in; after everything we have faced, I am in dire need of a drink.

The door from the captain's quarters creaks open, and I am happy to see Zerina emerge. She wears a grey, tattered blanket wrapped around her shoulders. Even though the sea air has ravaged her straight hair into a matted mass, she still looks enchanting.

Zerina offers me a sarcastic salute and I can't help but

grin. She wanders to the front of the ship, taking in the view ahead of us.

I steady the wheel and fix it into position so we can stay our true course, then join her at the bow. Her clothes look as battered as my own. Her green dress is torn and muddied, and the lower part of the dress is flattened against her body. I cannot help but appreciate her perfect form.

"Beautiful," I exhale, louder than I intend. "Erm, the sea," I quickly correct myself. "The view from here. It's beautiful." I feel my cheeks redden.

Zerina returns a smile before diverting her gaze back over the water. "It really is, isn't it. Where was it you learned how to man a ship?" She smiles playfully. "Stealing a boat, captaining a crew, running from the law. Are you sure this is the first time you have done this, Ulrik?"

I laugh. "I can safely say this is my first time turning to a life of piracy. In truth, I want nothing more to do with Levanthria, not that we can ever go back." The realisation weighs heavy on me. "Is it piracy to do what you need to protect those you love?"

All I'd wanted was to revitalize the vineyard and live peacefully with my family. I was done with the ocean. I know I can cope with a life at sea, but it remains to be seen whether Zerina and Esara will be able to. This is no life for a child. Esara will need to grow up quickly and keep her wits about her, especially when we make port.

"If that is the case, then I approve of you being a pirate. We just need to fix you up with a hat." Zerina's laughter is sweet, miles away from the furious enchantress I saw striking down our enemies in Eltera. It warms me. I have grown to appreciate her company.

Above, the cries of the gulls become louder. There are

many overhead, with some even beginning to land on the mast.

"We are near land," I muse.

"Good." Zerina spins and begins to walk away. I wonder if I did something to offend her, but then she looks over her shoulder, grinning. "Because you are in dire need of a bath, Ulrik." She moves in tandem with the waves, and I can't help but notice how well she has taken to this new life. Even in our dishevelled state, she is still a picture of beauty and serenity.

I almost skip back to the helm, more content than I have been for a while. I take hold of the wheel and hum to myself, fixing my gaze on the horizon as a mass of land materializes in the distance.

If we get things right in Voraz, the three of us might just have a future, and not one where we are merely surviving.

# 14
## ZERINA

"We will have to climb down, I am afraid. We lost the platform when we made our escape." Ulrik points to the thick rope that some boys below have tied to the pier of Voraz.

Ulrik goes first and makes it look easy, climbing down the rope with relative ease. Esara follows suit, albeit a little slower than her brother. The pier is busy with people passing up and down as they load a ship with cargo. The heat of the sun beams down on us, the warmth of the sun kissing my skin before a gentle breeze offers me a brief reprieve.

I try and mirror what the others have done, my heart racing. I've never climbed on a rope before. As I slowly edge down, I can hear the giggles of the boys on the docks. I swear I hear Ulrik and Esara too as I descend in the most unladylike manner. My dress grips the rope better than I do, and suddenly I find myself entangled.

Laughing, Ulrik holds out his hand, and when my skin touches his, I feel myself blush. With his assistance, my feet meet the pier, and I breathe a sigh of relief at not completely embarrassing myself by falling into the water.

As I brush my dress down, a woman approaches with a book open in her hands. She wears small spectacles that sit on the end of her nose, and her hair is long and greying.

"How long will you be making port here, sir?" She speaks as if she talks through her nose.

Ulrik takes a long look at the boat before turning back to the woman. "At least two weeks, good lady. We are in need of repairs and some bodies to form a crew."

"There's a tavern in town, The Two Shovels. You will find bodies there. Beretta is the ship smith over on the other side of the docks. She will help you with your repairs." She eyes Esara and me. "You best stay at the inns on the far side of town. There's less bother there. Can you tell me your name, sir, and that of your ship?" The woman fumbles around in her chest pocket before removing a quill, setting it against her book to record Ulrik's answers.

"My name is Ulrik, but I am afraid the ship has no name." Ulrik is truthful in his answers which surprises me. What if someone gives chase to us here?

"A nameless boat." The woman pauses her scribbling to examine the three of us through her tiny spectacles. "It's frightfully bad luck to sail on a ship that hasn't been given a name."

"So far it has brought us some good fortune." Ulrik smiles. "What do I owe?"

"Two weeks dock, that will be three crowns."

Ulrik rummages around in his satchel, then places some coins in the woman's hand.

The woman tips her head towards Ulrik. "Welcome to Voraz."

. . .

Bri once told me a story of sunshine and white beaches and bright green trees on southern islands, but despite the sun overhead, Voraz is dark and dank, lined with derelict buildings. A far cry from what I imagined.

There are so many people here. I can hear the blended noises of conversations, laughter, and arguments. As we make our way through the crowd, a man hands coin to a woman clothed in an elegant red dress and she leads him towards an alley. My mind is brought back to the man in Uster, and I feel shame. This woman does not appear to feel shame. Rather, she appears happy at the transaction, and I wonder what it must be like to not only give yourself freely, but to be in control of the situation.

"This way," Ulrik says.

We pass The Two Shovels where the noise is by far the rowdiest; I can hear shouts followed by the sound of glass smashing inside.

The smell of stale alcohol fills the streets, and a man lies sprawled out on the ground from intoxication, mumbling in his sleep. Another man sits slumped against the wall of a tavern, his clothes torn, his nose bloodied. A woman kneels by his side offering to tend to him, the dress she wears implying that she is perhaps soliciting something more tender.

It is only midmorning. I hate to see what state the town will be in come nightfall. We pass ramshackle shelters that seem to be scattered all over. Despite the brawling and the poverty, most appear to be in good spirits. It is a feeling I long to experience, but I still grieve for my sisters, so for now, happiness evades me.

It doesn't take us long to pass through Voraz and find the comfort of sandy beaches. I am taken aback by how you can go from such chaos to such serenity. The waves break as they hit the beach, and only a handful of people walk along the shore, admiring the view.

We find an inn that looks relatively well maintained compared to the others in Voraz. The back half of the building hides within large green trees that sway with the breeze. *This* is more like the stories.

"Last one there is a gnawbart!" Esara calls as she sets off at pace towards the inn.

Ulrik gives chase and Esara shrieks with laughter when he catches her and scoops her up in his arms. He looks back at me. "You heard her, Zerina. Last one there is a gnawbart." He sets off through the sand with Esara flung over his shoulder.

The playfulness brings a smile to my face, and I feel a slight pang of happiness as I give chase over the beach.

# 15

## ZERINA

'There is a difference between monsters and demons. Monsters have the ability to act on their own volition, demons attack and kill in frenzy without thought and mindless fury.'

*Kaya Niper, Former priestess of the temple of Eltera - 223 KR*

I leave Ulrik and Esara in our room and make my way down to a secluded part of the beach. The sound of the waves soothes my broken heart and I feel that I can gather my thoughts more clearly here and process everything that has happened. Everything is so different from when I lived in a small house barely able to survive the blistering winds that so regularly greeted us in the Pendaran Hills.

I removed my shoes, and although the hot sand initially feels as though it is burning my feet, I quickly become accustomed to it. Every step I take, I feel the sand in between my toes as I edge towards the water. Closing my eyes, I take in long deep breath and concentrate on my senses. I can hear the waves moving freely and untamed, the birds calling to one another as they scavenge for their meals from the ocean. I feel the heat of the sun against my body and the breath of the wind slowly cooling my skin. As I breathe slowly, the smell of the salt water softly greets me and I long to stay right here in this moment for as long as possible. A sharp coldness meets my feet as the shallow waves kiss my toes. The water is crisp and fresh, and sends my senses into overdrive before escaping away from me as the waves draw the water back.

I take a look around and see that the beach is empty, so I take the opportunity for a swim and to clean myself. I lower my gown and step out from it before throwing it further behind me where I hope that the waves do not steal them.

The sun beams down against my skin in its entirety now, and it relaxes me in an instant. The waves hit my feet again, and I begin to run towards the water. It takes my breath away when it hits me, but it is exhilarating as I embrace the power that the water holds. Submerging myself in the water, and all sound disappears. I wait in anticipation, praying to the gods that I will hear my sister's voice once more. No voice arrives, and I find my air running short. Kicking my legs, I reach the surface and take in the fresh air, pausing to appreciate the warmth of the sun against my skin. I inhale deeply before submerging myself under the water once again. I suspend myself in the ocean, and I feel calm and collecting waiting in anticipation for another message from Lyrissa.

Moments pass. A few seconds feels like much longer under water. My mind flashes back to being forced into the barrel of water in Eltera, but I quickly steady myself. I hear nothing, no words of comfort or direction, and a pain stabs at my heart like a sharpened blade. My heart begins to beat faster and faster and I swear for a moment I hear the beats pulsating through me. I contemplate staying here, letting the ocean have me. I could be with my sisters once again in the afterlife.

As the air in my lungs diminishes, I do not panic. If anything, it feels exhilarating. Lost in the moment, the disappointment of not hearing my sister's voice is replaced with a strong sense of purpose. Lyrissa gave me a vision. Somehow she communicated with me from the afterlife and that has brought us here to Voraz. I have to fight, I have to find what it is my sister points me towards. My chest beats wildly as my body runs short of air and I kick my legs, searching for the surface once more, the distorted shape of the sun rippling above me.

A form moves towards me and takes hold of my outstretched wrists, and I find myself being pulled upwards. As my head breaches the water, I breathe in as big of a gasp of air as I can muster. It has never tasted so sweet as it does on this day. I embrace the warmth that the sun instantly provides my face before beginning to thrash around ungracefully; I have swam out farther than I intended.

"Zerina! Zerina!" Ulrik grips me tightly as he brings me back to the shallower waters where I steady myself. He grips me tightly against him until he is confident that I am able to tread water by myself. "Are you able to swim?"

"What are you doing?" I am panting like a dog through lack of air.

"Were you not in difficulty?" his face is a picture of worry.

"I was swimming. I thought that if I stayed under the water for long enough, I might hear my sister's voice again." I am suddenly engulfed by the realisation that I am wearing no clothes, and I spin myself away from Ulrik, not wanting to reveal myself any more than I already have.

"Sorry, I thought you were struggling, I didn't mean any offence." Ulrik fumbles his words awkwardly before averting his eyes. "I'll just, sorry, I didn't see anything."

We float in the water, weightless and bobbing in the waves the heat of the sun beating down on us.

"I only jumped in because I saw you suddenly drop under the water. When you didn't return for air, I thought you needed help."

"It's okay."

We continue to tread water, an uncomfortable silence building between us.

"Let's go get some breakfast," Ulrik breaks the silence and he begins to swim back to the shore.

Looking out at the expanse of water, I ponder how far it reaches, and I feel insignificant in comparison to how big the world is. What I would give to hear my dear Lyrissa's voice one more time, to be able to have a simple conversation. I let out a huge sigh, giving one last look at the water, the waves rippling under the light of the sun.

Ulrik has already reached the beach and is heading back to dry off. I swim slowly back to the sand myself, knowing that I will be able to keep what remains of my dignity intact without showing every part of me to Ulrik. Covering myself as I reach waters shallow enough to walk, I move quickly to grab my dress and pull it over me.

I glance out at the water which just nearly swallowed me. There are only two people on this world now that care I exist, and my thoughts remain with my fallen sisters. I notice Esara waving me over to some food she has prepared on a makeshift table on the beach. She is so innocent. I only hope that this place does not taint her. For now, I just want to enjoy this moment.

# 16

## ULRIK

Work hard trading all day, drink and fight all night, wake early, and repeat. Life in Voraz isn't for me, but I would be lying if I said I was not ready for a good drink, a way to numb the mind and quell the memory of my mother's severed head. But that must wait.

The morning market is already alive and ready for the day, though clearly the market vendors had some late nights, judging by the rough expressions on their faces. One vendor drops a small crate of fruit, and he sways like he might still be drunk as he tries to gather up the oranges rolling away.

Maybe I'll buy one from him later but right now, my focus is on survival.

After bumping through the crowd, I finally find a weaponsmith. She stoops in her chair, bottle of rum in hand, and her dull blond hair is matted over her face.

I fake a cough to startle the woman awake. She stirs, making all kinds of unnatural noises as she rises from her drunken stupor.

"What ye want, ye yarwool!" she splutters, reaching for a hammer by her side. Her eyes roll around wildly as she takes in the light of the day, her world still spinning.

I raise both my hands to show that I mean no harm. "I'm just here to get some supplies. You are a weaponsmith, aren't you?"

She fixes me with her dark eyes, looking me up and down before she offers me a smile. "Handsome one, ain't ya."

I shudder and hope that she does not expect favours for her weapons.

"I have coin. Please miss, show me your wares." I cringe. Maybe I should have worded that differently.

She grins, showing off her dirty teeth, two of which are missing. "I'll show ya more than that if you want." Suddenly I feel like prime cut of meat.

Ignoring her, I direct my gaze to the table beside her and see exactly what I am looking for. There are all manner of weapons on the table; a mace, sword, bow and arrows, lined up like a metallic buffet. They seem in good condition when I examine them more closely.

"I'll take dagger and small sword." The sword looks like a good fit for Zerina.

"Two silver coins for the dagger, and a gold coin for the sword." The woman heaves as she stops herself from being sick, and I wonder how on earth she has survived Voraz this long.

The price seems steep but I nod and do the transaction.

"Feel free t' come back if ye need anything else," the woman teases, winking.

I force a polite smile before making my escape. The smell of ale and warm bread fills the streets, and I find the two fragrances work well together. My stomach rumbles with the encouragement of the freshly baked bread, and I look forward to getting back to have breakfast with Esara and Zerina.

My mind jumps to her naked form in the ocean from this morning. More than anything I hope she does not think I was ogling her whilst she bathed. I shake thoughts of her form out of my head.

I cannot afford such distractions. My focus needs to be on the three of us surviving, and on finding that cave.

# 17

## ZERINA

'*There is stories of a man, driven initially by greed. The people of Askela followed him to the Forest of Opiya. It is here where he made a camp and from here where he has taught them how to survive.'*

*Anonymous note - 261 KR*

"How was your swim?" Esara grins at me with wide eyes. She sits peeling a fibrous orange then bites into it, savouring the flavour.

"It was . . ." I pause. Despite Ulrik's misunderstanding that led to me being rescued in the most undignified way, I found the way he leapt to my aid it endearing. "Nice," I answer as I pull my damp hair from behind me to rest over my shoulder. The breeze catches the back of my neck, causing the skin on my arms to rise.

"I saw you both," Esara continues, still smiling. "In the water."

"That isn't what you think, Esara. Your brother thought I was in difficulty in the water."

"Yeah, yeah," she teases, raising her eyebrows. "I'm not a child. I know what happens between two adults."

My cheeks burn like the sun. "Esara, I have no idea what you mean." I do not know how to respond, but I can't help but muster a deft smile.

Esara drops me a sceptical look.

For the most part, I feel embarrassment. I have never shown any part of me to a man, and had always thought that when it happened it would not be under circumstances like these.

My stomach churns with hunger, and one of the apples on the table in front of me stands out.

"There's no need to wait, Ulrik will not mind."

My sisters always taught me to wait until everyone was at the table before eating.

Esara grins and takes a kulo fruit, cracking open its green exterior before bringing the juices to her face. She slurps the insides, then pulls it away with a childish grin, the juices running from her mouth.

"Esara," I tease, "show some decorum."

"There's no need for civility here, Zerina." She passes me the bright red apple.

I hesitate, but we both hear my stomach growl. I grab it and bite into it as if I am a wild thing that hasn't eaten for days. The crisp juice of the apple is refreshing in this morning heat, and the sweetness causes the upper part of my cheek to sting slightly. I care not for the gormless grin I have plastered over my face as I chew.

Then something moves from within, and my stomach instantly ties up in knots. I feel as though I will heave as a worm pushes its way through a rotten hole, its slimy body poking out as if seeking the sun. I spit it out and begin to cough, reaching for the cup of water in front of me.

Esara giggles uncontrollably at my misfortune, and the thought that she may have done this purposely runs through my mind.

"Esara, did you not check the fruit?" I scold, my pangs of hunger quickly changing to frustration. Suddenly I am not in the mood for food.

Esara's giggles stop, and she looks upset by my scolding, her hands dropping to her knees.

Guilt instantly washes over me like a splash of cold water, and I know in my heart she would not do such a thing intentionally. "I'm sorry, it's just . . ."

"It's okay, Zerina, I can fix it."

She takes the worm-addled apple, delicately plucks the worm that has taken up residence, and throws it over her shoulder before clasping the apple with both hands. I gasp as a gentle glow flashes in between her palms. She opens her hands to reveal a perfectly formed apple, devoid of rot.

"Esara, you can use magic?"

"Don't tell Ulrik. He doesn't approve." She stretches out her, offering it to me.

"How?" I assumed the accusation against her at the trial was a false allegation.

"My mum taught me how to control it when we were not able to afford the ingredients to stop my powers from surfacing. Things were really hard when Ulrik left. It's the only power I have." Esara's thoughts seem to wander, and I know she's thinking about her mother.

"You can heal things?" I pray it isn't necromancy; no one should be able to manipulate death and decay.

Esara shakes her head. "It's a glamour," she whispers, though there is no one around at this early hour. "The apple is the same apple which you had bitten. It will taste the same too. I have just changed its appearance."

Although tempted to eat the beautiful looking apple, I place it back on the table, unable to banish the thoughts of another worm greeting me.

Esara retrieves another apple from the table and her hands once again glow from underneath, beads of light escaping through her fingertips. When she removes them, a kulo fruit sits where the apple was.

"Go on, try it, you will understand then." Esara passes the fruit to me.

After my last experience I am apprehensive to bite into it, but I am curious about the magic that Esara wields. Picking up the fruit, I notice the skin feels rough to the touch like that of a ripened kulo, and not smooth as an apple is. My heart skips in surprise and I feel excited about what Esara has done. To my surprise it, tastes just like an apple, though the texture is different, and the inside is as soft as a kulo.

"I can only manipulate the appearance of something. Everything else remains the same," Esara explains.

I feel like Esara has schooled me today, despite her younger years.

"This is a gift, Esara, but please be careful using magic," I tell her, thinking of Lyrissa's affliction.

Her smile turns into sadness, and I feel guilty for taking her moment away from her.

"My mum always said that. But what harm can casting a glamour do, really?"

"I presume your mother taught you about the addiction that magic brings?"

"Yes, she did, but I just don't understand why we can't use my magic to help us."

"That feeling you have right now – that sense that you are full of energy, that nothing can stop you – that is the magic. When you use it, you get a feeling of excitement. Like in that moment, you are invincible."

"I could turn some sand into gold coins. We wouldn't have to worry about anything. We could live in luxury!"

I shake my head. "My sister, Lyrissa, started off using her magic to hunt for food. We found out, but by that point she was unable to stop. The addiction had taken her. I had to watch her writhe in pain, and each time our backs were turned, she summoned that little bit of magic to dampen her agony. First her mind began to go, then her body. By the time she reached her twenty-first birthday, she looked as though she was forty. By the time she was twenty-five, sixty."

Esara refuses to look at me as a I speak.

I reach for her hands, pulling her closer. "Promise me that you will not use this magic again. And that if you are to do it, it is only if your life is in immediate danger."

Esara's eyes well and she nods silently.

All I can do is hope my sister's story resonates with her and pray that it is enough. No one is powerful enough to resist the addiction of magic.

# 18

## ULRIK

When I arrive, Esara and Zerina appear deep in conversation about something. Sweat pools on my face from the walk, but the markets have proved to have exactly what we needed. I clutch the weapons I acquired in one hand, and hold fresh clothes that I purchased over my shoulder.

My coin purse is a lot lighter than I would have liked, but we still have enough to trade for food for at least a few weeks if we use it sparingly. For now, surviving on what we have is our only option. We have managed this long, despite the barriers we have already faced. I see no other option other than to follow the map we marked based on Zerina's vision, in the hope that the rewards for what awaits us there will help us.

I banish thoughts of finding a chest full of treasure; that kind of find simply doesn't happen. If every pirate found treasure so easily, why are there so many in Voraz sitting in drunken stupor? Why are so many men and women who turn to piracy so skinny and dishevelled, their skin cracked and broke, their teeth decaying? Such a find is nothing more than a dream, something to get people to turn to piracy with false hopes about the riches that lie in wait for anyone bold enough to search for it.

As I approach Esara and Zerina, it feels as though stronger words have been spoken. Zerina wipes her eyes.

"Everything okay?" I ask, curious as to what could have happened in my absence. Zerina's eyes meet my own and again my mind goes back to her in the ocean.

"We're fine. I was just telling Esara a story about my sisters," she explains. "Unfortunately they have brought back some painful memories." She stifles back further tears and forces a smile.

"What have you got there?" Esara cuts in, diverting my attention. Her sweet smile is all I need to see on any day to keep me motivated. I have spent far too many years away from her and I will never do such a thing again.

I drop the clothes onto the table. "I had to guess your sizes, but you will fare far better with this than the dresses that you are wearing."

Esara grins at me like a court jester. "I'm not interested in the clothes. What are those?" She points to the weapons.

"This," I say, "is a way to protect yourself." I place the small sword and dagger on top of the clothes. "Without needing to use magic." My eyes drift to Zerina. I have seen the aftereffects on her body from wielding such a raw force. I do not wish to see Esara go through the same. Her magic may be suppressed for now, but I will also need to make our mother's recipe to keep her safe and stop her powers from manifesting.

I pass the small sword and holster to Zerina and smile at her. "This one is for you."

She gives a timid smile and nods in appreciation before taking the sword from me. For a moment, our fingers touch. "Why, thank you, kind sir." She feigns a curtsy and casts me another smile, this one more confident. "But I have never used one before. I have never needed such an item."

"I can teach you!" Esara squeals, ready to explode with excitement.

I cannot help but laugh at her eagerness. "And where have you learnt to fight?" I ruffle her already matted hair with my hand, causing it to fall in front of her face.

"I taught myself." Then her eyes latch onto the blade like a shark targeting its prey. "Is that for me?" Her eyes are so wide, I worry they might pop out.

"You assume this is for you?" I tease. "Yes, it is for you." I pass her the blade.

"Thank you, thank you, thank you!" she exclaims. "I love you, Ulrik." She dives from the table and unsheathes the dagger without hesitation. She begins to prod, poke, and jab at the air while making noises as if she is fighting an enemy. "Take that!"

Zerina and I share a laugh as she continues her fight against the unknown enemy.

"You will need to train every day, Esara. Hopefully you will never have to use it." I pray she will be much older when the time comes for her to use that dagger, but with the world the way it is, I know deep down that the day will come sooner rather than later.

"Ah," I say, picking up the kulo fruit on the table, "nothing better than a fresh kulo fruit."

Esara stops in her tracks, then runs at me and knocks the fruit out of my hand.

"What are you playing at, Esara? I'm starving!"

Zerina quickly stands to defend her, the two of them suddenly acting strange. "She only means to help you," she tells me, putting a protective arm across Esara as if I mean to hurt her.

"If she behaves in this manner, she will not get a scolding from me. She is still a child after all, a child under my ward." I feel my chest puff up and my frustrations grow at their behaviour.

"The fruit is rotten, that is all," Zerina says. "Just a few moments ago I bit into an apple which had a worm in it Esara only means to stop you eating rotten fruit." Her words are a bit over-zealous for my liking.

"Why not simply tell me that then, Esara, rather than attacking me like an enraged scamp?"

Esara snatches her clothing from the table. "I won't bother next time. You can eat all the rotten fruit you want." She storms off towards the inn, stamping her feet into the sand.

"She was merely helping you, Ulrik."

"Do not tell me how to school my sister," I snap.

Zerina stares deeply at me for a moment, then turns to leave.

"Zerina I am sorry, I didn't mean – "

"I am *not* your sister, and I do not need schooling." She sets off across the sand in Esara's wake.

In a matter of seconds, I have managed to make the two of them fall out with me over something as trivial as eating a kulo fruit. I look at the fruit which sits encased in the sand it has been knocked into.

I can't help but feel this whole thing has been an over-reaction.

# 19

## ZERINA

'How many times has man disappointed the gods that provide the very air that they breathe. Time and time again they manage to out do themselves, even by their own low standards. I would go as far to say that is man who are the real monsters of this earth.'

*Zaphire Etsom, The Temple Of Eltera - 257 KR*

The clothes that Ulrik fetched fit me well, and I tuck my white blouse into linen pants, eying myself in a dirty mirror. Having grown up wearing dresses, it feels unnatural to wear trousers, but I do understand the reasoning for them.

Now I pace in my chamber like a caged animal. I don't know why I feel such frustration towards Ulrik for his reaction about the kulo fruit, but I also do not understand why Esara would want to hide her magic from him.

It shocked me to see Ulrik react the way he did. Then to scold me in such a manner – it was uncalled for.

I stop pacing and gather my thoughts. Have I been

mistaken about Ulrik? Maybe my path lies elsewhere. Maybe I need to walk away and take my chances on my own. I shake my head at the thought, knowing I am kidding no one.

I would not last five minutes on my own. This is just a minor disagreement. Surely it means nothing more?

There is a light tap on the door, too soft for it to be Ulrik.

"Door's open," I call out.

Esara steps into the room and I am taken aback by her appearance. Like me, she wears trousers and a blouse, and her dagger is clipped onto a leather belt around her waist. Brown boots travel to her knees, and her vibrant blond hair is tied back and held into place under a bandana. She could easily pass as a boy as she stands before me, nothing but her distinguished freckles giving her away. She beams at me and I wonder what has caught her in such a fine mood.

"I think it worked," she says with a grin.

"What worked?"

"Is your memory that bad, Zerina? Out there, that little show I put on for my brother? I think it distracted him from the glamoured apple."

"So you're not upset with him?"

"Nope." She looks herself over, then gives me a playful twirl. "What do you think of my disguise?"

I am surprised. The girl put on a show worthy of the theatre. I was convinced that she was furious with Ulrik about the way he had spoken to her. "You do know your brother and I had an argument when I defended you?" I ask, annoyed.

Esara's soft, innocent smile would soften the hardest of hearts. "Zerina, you need to learn how to be with him. He's a hothead at times, but he only wants to protect us. Watch when he sees us; he will be racked with guilt for how he has spoken, and he'll tell us both how sorry he is."

"Esara, I am shocked by the way you manipulated him. Where is he?"

"No idea. Probably pacing around his room cursing us, but he was away from me too long with the navy to stay mad at me. Besides, I am his little sister." She flutters her eyes at me, the epitome of innocence.

There is another knock at the door. Whilst it is firmer, than Esara's, there is a delicateness to it.

"Yes?" I call out, joining Esara's act by feigning frustration.

Ulrik pushes the door open and stands in the doorway looking sheepish. He holds his new hat in his hands, fumbling the edge of it between his fingers awkwardly. "Good, you're both here." He clears his throat. "I just wanted to say that I am sorry for earlier. I did not mean to speak to you in such a manner." He pauses for a moment. "Either of you."

His eyes meet mine and for a moment, I lose myself in their darkness. I feel guilt for him coming to us in such a way when this whole situation has been manipulated by his sister.

Esara gives me a coy, told-you-so look, then faces Ulrik. "Don't do it again, Ulrik. You really upset me." I am amazed at how easy she finds it, the lying.

Ulrik opens his arms to invite Esara in for a hug, an invitation which she accepts straight away. "I am sorry, sister."

Esara looks back over her shoulder, casting me another smile.

"What is the plan today?" I interrupt.

"We go inland, to the depths of the trees. According to

your vision, that is where this cave lies," Ulrik says, pulling away from Esara.

"It could be a complete waste of time," I murmur, worrying that we are chasing shadows. The last thing I want is to send us on a wild goose chase.

"Your sister is guiding you there, is she not?" Ulrik removes his coin purse and gives it a shake. "I have enough coin to last us little over a week. There must be a reason you have seen this cave, a sign from the gods. I – I don't know what else to do."

On two occasions now, I have heard Lyrissa's words as if she guides me. Is this a madness induced by using magic?

"Okay," I say. "When do we leave?"

# 20

## ULRIK

I swing my sword through the dense trees to clear a path. The humidity is harsh, and my shirt sticks to me like a wet cloth.

"Brother, must we continue?" Esara whines for the hundredth time.

"We need to make haste if we are to be out of these trees by nightfall. Who knows what manner of creatures will come out of the shadows?" In truth, I know not what beasts live in this place, but I hope my words give Esara the inspiration she needs to keep going. Casting a glance over my shoulder, I see her eyes franticly search through the thick trees.

Zerina walks behind Esara, hacking through the remaining overgrowth with her short sword. Her hair is tied back, and with her new wardrobe, I think the look suits her. My eyes linger for a moment before she meets my gaze. I quickly spin to look ahead once more.

"Ulrik, I need a drink," Esara fumes. I can tell from her tone that I am not going to get much more from her if we do not take a short rest.

"Fine, we can stop, but only for a moment."

Her cheeks are bright red, and out of the three of us, she is sweating the most.

"You have done well keeping face, sister." I ruffle her head to tease her as she reaches for her water bottle and begins to gulp its contents down. "Woah, don't drink it all, Esara. You must ration it."

Esara ignores me and continues to drink. She lets out a sigh when she finishes her bottle. "That's fine, Ulrik. If I get thirsty again, you will just give me yours." She gives me a smug smile because she knows she is right.

She reminds me of myself when I was that age.

"How do we even know that we are moving in the right direction?" Zerina asks before taking a swig out of her own flask. She is panting heavily.

"A combination of luck and using the sun's location to keep us on track." I point towards the skies but the tree canopies above are beginning to get thick enough to block out the light.

"Wait," Zerina's voice elevates.

I wonder if she has spotted a wild beast in the midst of the trees, and my hand slides to my sword.

"Something feels familiar, like I have been here before." She stops in her tracks and takes in our surroundings. "I am sure of it."

Zerina searches around us, and Esara drags herself back to her feet, excited with the prospect of finding this cave. I can only pray that when we do find it, there is something of value for us to collect. I move to the thick leaves and vines that block our route and begin hacking once more.

Sparks fly when my sword hits something solid.

My heart skips. Could Zerina's vision really be true after all?

"We are here!" Zerina exclaims. "We just need to find the entrance!"

When I place my hand against the rock surface, the coldness of the stone cools my hand. Esara and Zerina join me and begin to remove the vines, a newfound energy coming from all three of us.

The vines pile on the floor as we continue to hack and chop them down.

"I think I've found something!" Esara squeals, revealing a darkened space within the thick vegetation. I yank the vines down to clear larger opening. To the right, my attention is grabbed by a strange indentation in the stone. It is as if a hand has forced itself into the rock face.

"I have seen that," Zerina whispers. "I saw the mage who created it." She runs her fingers over the handprint. "You have done it, Esara!" She hugs Esara tightly.

Esara's face brightens from the praise as she stares into the dark void.

The light behind us barely enters the cave, stopping within a meter of the entrance. Tentatively, I take the first step inside. It is impossible to see a path inside, and I remove some ripped clothing that I have brought with me for such an occasion.

"Zerina, pass me a thick branch," I ask. She quickly looks around her for something suitable. Within a moment she has passed one to me, and I wrap the fabric around the top, then pour oil over it to create a torch. I take out flint and steel from my satchel, and strike them together, forcing a spark. Soon, our immediate space is illuminated.

"Keep behind me," I command the other two.

My heart beats a little bit faster as I move towards the darkness.

# 21

## ZERINA

'The world is a mysterious place, I have seen many a monster, many a creature walk these plains. I have lost count of how many I have freed from their curse, only with their death can it truly be broken.'
*Diary of the monster hunter Gregor Yerald - 253 KR*

My chest feels like it is about to explode as we follow Ulrik deeper into the cave. The air is musty and tastes damp as I breathe at an accelerated rate. Esara clings to the back of her brother, trying to burrow her head into his back. The flame on his torch flickers and crackles slightly but the torch shows no signs of fading, much to my relief. The hairs on the back of my arms rise as I shudder at the thought of navigating this cave in the pitch black.

I move right behind Esara, the light from Ulrik's torch only just surrounding the three of us. With each step we take, I fear waking a hibernating creature or triggering some form of trap. My legs tremble as we descend into the depths of this cave. I should have just waited outside.

Ulrik's bravery overshadows my own, and I feel more of a hindrance than a help.

The sound of our footsteps echoes inside the walls, the dirt on the ground crunching underfoot. We do not talk, we simply move. I pray that the darkness does not last forever, for every step that we take, a newfound fear of the shadows creeps into my soul.

A wall of musty air hits me from the front, and the vile taste causes me to cough. The echo is much larger than before, and I realise we have hit a larger cavern.

Above, a large beam of light finds its way through. Never have I been so grateful to see natural light. It cuts through the darkness like a blade, illuminating dust that floats around in the air.

"There's something there, look!" Esara points to where the beam of light reaches a small island of dirt surrounded by water. "Is that a skeleton?"

We approach the water's edge that surrounds the patch of dirt. A form sits, slumped in the centre of the island. The light only reveals what looks like a skeletal hand.

"How long do you think he's been down here?" Esara asks.

"Long enough for his skin to turn to ash," I answer. I can only pray that a similar fate does not befall us.

As we approach, Ulrik stretches out his arm to stop us from wading into the shallow water that has pooled around the small island.

"Only one of us should cross in case it is some form of trap," he begins. "I will go across." He passes me the torch.

As I take hold of it, I am surprised at the heat that I can feel on my cheeks from the flame. I grip it tightly and hold it as far away as I can.

The splash of Ulrik entering the water echoes loudly. If

there is anything else living in this cave, it will surely know we are here now. I hear Ulrik gasp for breath; the water must be cold.

He disappears into a patch of darkness, out of reach from the beam of light coming from the ceiling. Within a couple of seconds, he emerges again and approaches the island in the centre, looking taller as he slowly rises from the water. Ulrik stops and stands over the skeleton, then reaches down slowly and pulls something from its hand that appears to be a roll of parchment. He places it inside his jacket.

"There's nothing here other than this skeleton and the parchment," he calls over to us. "Wait – " he kneels down and pulls something over the skeleton's head, and starts stripping its fingers of the rings that it wears. "We will be able to barter with this jewellery," he says, pocketing the trinkets.

"Ulrik!" Esara shouts, causing me to jump. "Something is moving towards you from the water!" She points franticly to the darkened patches within the cave.

I have been so transfixed on Ulrik that I did not notice the ripples taking form in the water. Shadows begin to rise from its depths. At first glance I count three, but I can't make out what they are.

"Look out!" Esara shouts.

The skeletal hand reaches to grab hold of Ulrik's leg.

"Skeletons!" I call. "The skeleton isn't dead!"

Ulrik darts out of the way as the skeleton swipes at him. He draws his sword, and three more skeletons rise towards him from the water's edge, closing in.

The skeleton that already accompanies him on the island clamours to its feet as if being pulled by strings like a puppet. My blood runs cold. It clasps a sword in its hand.

"Ulrik!" I yell.

It takes a swipe at Ulrik who quickly manages to parry it away.

"Go!" Ulrik shouts as he begins to trade blows with the skeleton. The others reach the island with their swords and spears pointed towards him.

As much as I want to follow Ulrik's order, I know in my heart that we can't leave him. I pass Esara the torch and without thinking, I wade into the water. The cold stabs into my legs like needles but I have little time to think.

"Esara, stay there! If anything comes near you, you run, okay?"

The other skeletons reach Ulrik before I can get to the island, and I am surprised at how fast they move. Their joints do not move as they should. Their knees and arms look as though they could snap and break at any moment as they flex unnaturally without any skin or sinew to hold them into place. One of them tries to impale Ulrik with a spear but Ulrik grabs the shaft, then rolls the weapon and strikes the skeleton's head with his blade.

With a sickening snap, the skeleton's head jerks sideways as its neck cracks, hanging at an unnatural angle. The ailment does not deter the undead warrior, however, and it drags its spear back from Ulrik's hand and attempts to impale him once more. This time, Ulrik only just manages to move himself out of the way before another skeleton takes a swipe at him.

I press through the water quickly, the task getting easier as I begin to rise from the depths. I draw my blade and splash towards Ulrik. One of the skeletons notices me and switches its focus from Ulrik. It raises its sword and brings it down upon me, and instinctively, I pull my weapon around to shield myself from the blow.

For something that is not living, its strength shocks me. I have never wielded a bade, not even to practice, and the vibration of metal on metal almost causes me to drop my sword.

"Zerina, what are you doing?" Ulrik scolds me as he continues to fight off our attackers.

"Saving you," I fire back as I parry away another strike from the skeleton.

The two of us end up back-to-back as the four skeletons circle us. Their bones grind and their teeth chatter. We manage to keep them at bay, but it doesn't take long before my arms begin to tire. Each time I swing, my sword feels a little bit heavier.

"How do you kill something that is already dead?" Ulrik gasps, his breath growing laboured.

"By using something unnatural," I answer. It is a bad choice, but I see no other option. I focus myself and feel my hands begin to warm as I summon the magic from within me.

As my hands glow, I can see the skeletons around us in their full, gruesome forms. The ones that have been in the water are covered in moss and algae. Their bones shimmer in the light that my magic brings. They hesitate as I draw upon my power, but it is too late for them. I wave my hands and flames begin to wrap around Ulrik and me, forming a shield between us and them. My legs feel as though they may buckle, but I continue to summon the magic with everything I have.

I have never used it in this way, but somehow, I know what I need to do. I raise my hands from below me to above, as if conducting an orchestra. The flames rise with my motion; they are under my control now. I fix my eyes on one of the skeletons and push my hand towards it. The flames engulf it, and a piercing shriek fills the cavern as the skeleton crumples to the floor.

I spin and swipe my hands in a circle, dancing around Ulrik as my flames begin to destroy the decayed bones that mean to kill us. I feel euphoric as the magic courses through me, as if I am a master at casting spells, as if I could destroy a hundred skeletons with ease.

The aches in my arms and legs leave as a freshness runs through my veins like the ocean washing the beach with its cascading waves. I feel energised, like I can hold on to this magic for as long as I need to. The skeletons wail and shriek as my magic engulfs them in their entirety, flailing and writhing on the floor.

A muffled noise fills my ears but it takes a few moments before I realise that it is Ulrik.

"Zerina, Zerina!" His words slowly dampen, and he is able to cut through to me. "Let's go!"

My magic fades and the flames around us disappear. Then a cold, sharp sensation runs up my arms as though ice has replaced my blood.

Ulrik rushes into the water and I quickly follow, not wishing to remain on the island on my own. We reach the other side and a pale-looking Esara struggles to form words with what she has just seen. She points to the water. More skeletons are appearing, creeping from the shadows.

"How many are there?" I ask. My arms are in agony from the magic that I have used, and I do not know if I have it in me to summon more.

"I do not wish to wait around and see!" Ulrik shakes Esara who continues to stare out at the water as if she is in shock. "Come on, Esara, we need to go! Head back the way we came, go!" Ulrik grabs my arm and pulls me level with Esara to send us on our way. "Go!"

More skeletons move towards us, and he begins to duel with the first two. They are clumsy and not as agile with a sword as Ulrik. He slices off one of their arms before kicking another to the ground, then spins to follow. He gives me a look that tells me he will not ask us to move again.

I oblige and tail Esara out of the cavern and down the winding tunnels that led us here. She moves quickly for such a young girl. My legs are leaden, each step causing more and more discomfort, but I push through the pain as we search for the entrance. My heart is pumping and I am short of breath, but I keep going. I do not wish to wait and see what the skeleton defenders would do to us. The last thing I want is to become cursed like they are, bound to protect this place.

"There it is!" Esara calls as she seeks to guide us out of the cave. "We are nearly there."

With a thud, she hits the ground, skidding through the dirt. She lets out a cry as she grinds to a stop. I grab the back of her top and pull her to her feet as fast as possible, then Ulrik reaches us and scoops the two of us up together.

Behind us, the skeletons draw closer, their bones clicking wildly as they give chase. The light grows ever closer, and I push past the burning sensation in my legs, though I feel they will give way at any moment. We reach the entrance and I push Esara forward with as much might as I can muster. I throw myself out of the cave after her, then spin around, ready to fight.

In a matter of seconds, the skeletons are upon us. I raise my sword, shoving Esara behind me.

As soon as they leave the boundaries of the cave, though, their bones collapse in heaps, as if the magic tethering them together has vanished.

More skeletons stop at the entrance to the cave, staring at us as we form a defensive line.

I breathe a sigh of relief. They cannot follow us.

"We shouldn't take any chances," Ulrik says, continuing towards the trees. "We need to make it back before dark, and I do not wish to wait and see if they find a way out of that cave."

We got what we came for. Now we need to get back to the shoreline, and find out why Lyrissa sent us here.

# 22

## ULRIK

Arriving out of the dense trees, I drop to my knees and let my hands sink into the warm sand. My breathing is heavy and I'm in dire need of a rest after today's antics. Never have I witnessed such magic, such ferocity. Not only in the skeletons that tried to kill us, but in the fires that Zerina summoned to keep us safe.

I let the sand slide over my fingertips. We are safe. We got what we wanted.

Esara lies on the ground face first, catching her breath. She looks like a bear rug that sits in front of an open fire as she pants heavily. Zerina steadies herself against a palm tree, heaving into the nearby bushes. Whether that is from the magic or all the running remains to be seen.

Esara rolls onto her back and stares up at the setting sky, her face blemished with cuts and grazes.

"Are you okay, sister?" I offer her my hand as well as my water bottle.

"You never said anything about skeletons, Ulrik!" she tells me off as if I am the child in this relationship before accepting my hand and snatching the water bottle from me. Sweat falls from her face as she empties my flask. Luckily we are not far from the inn, so I know I will be able to get some water soon enough. As long as Esara is okay, I am okay.

I have been naive in the danger that I have placed her in, and for that I feel the weight of guilt.

"Do we have anything stronger than water?" Zerina splutters in between throwing up the contents of her stomach. "I hope there is something of value on that parchment you found."

"The rings will fetch us some coin or allow us to barter for goods," I explain, all the while wondering if the danger we have just been through will be worth it.

I remove the stained, musty fabric that I took from the skeleton. It is rolled up with a large ring of metal holding it in place. It is made out of a material I am not familiar with, thin like parchment yet the feel of leather. The stench of death and decay cling to it like an unwanted blanket.

I carefully slide off the metal ring, then unroll the parchment piece. There are some holes where insects and creatures have feasted on the material, but I am still able to make out the contents clearly: a detailed drawing of a chalice is blotted inside, with inscriptions written underneath it that I do not understand.

"What is it?" Zerina asks as she makes her way over to me, the colour drained from her face and her features stretched and gaunt.

"It's a drawing. I can't make out what the words are." I squint as I try to read the words aloud: "*in cectelë-o nessë.*" My northern accent makes the words roll off my tongue like a lump of coal.

"Sounds Elvish." Zerina gestures to take the map from me. "Please let me see."

I pass her the map in disbelief. The Elvish language has not been used for hundreds of years, not since the Elvish people of Quinara were thought to have died out. If verified, the drawing with the Elvish scribing would potentially fetch a price that would allow us to live comfortably for months.

"How do you know it is Elvish?"

"*In cectelë-o nessë.*" Zerina's softly spoken voice suits the words as she repeats them with far more elegance than I could ever muster.

"Can you read Elvish? How?" I cannot believe it. Of all the chances, to have one of us able to read the words.

"I've never seen Elvish writing before," says Esara, creeping over Zerina's shoulder to catch a glimpse.

Zerina's dark, tired eyes look up from the drawing. Sadness lies within them. "My sisters taught me. They believed it was linked to mastering the magic that flows through us. Bri used to tell me that our mother was a descendant of an elf. I can only think that Elvish magic would be powerful enough to not only resurrect the dead, but to last so long without fading."

"What does it say?" I respond, trying not to sound too eager as I imagine the coin we could sell this for.

She pauses, checking her reading before speaking aloud. "'The' is the first word. The last word is definitely 'youth'. It also makes reference to 'Treventine.'"

My legs almost give way from underneath me, but I just manage to keep myself standing. "The fountain of youth!" I speak in almost a whisper, not believing the words that Zerina ushers. "It can't be. Such a thing is a myth, an old wives' tale to keep men at sea motivated." My words stutter, a state of disbelief coming over me. "And it's in Treventine?"

Zerina smiles. "It would seem so."

"We have what we need to make the biggest discovery this land has ever known," I tell her, unable to contain my excitement.

"Never mind that," Esara chimes in. "Will it make us rich? And will it mean the king and his soldiers will not want us dead?"

"If this is true and leads us to the fountain of youth, we will never need to run again, dear sister." I laugh and scoop her up, dancing around.

"What do we do next?" Zerina asks. She is somewhat less enthused than me, but she looks as though she could fall asleep standing up.

"You need to rest, and I need to find us some men and women to help us. We will need a crew." A new wave of energy courses through me like a rallying steed.

"Where do you plan on finding them at such short notice?" Zerina quizzes, sceptical at my plan.

"My dear Zerina, we are in Voraz. There are plenty of pirates here who will be mad enough to join us."

And I know just the place.

# 23

## ULRIK

'The boy astounds me every day, with every hardship that we face. Laith's ability to always put others before himself is a trait not shown enough in this cruel world. We head to Zakron, my dreams tell me we must search the tombs of the forgotten kings. It is here where I think we will find it, where we will find the sword in the stone.'

Letter from Jordell to Vireo - 262 KR

The moon sits low, illuminating the path into town.

Outside The Two Shovels, the combined noise of rowdy men and women full of ale are dampened by the windows and doors. One of the windows is boarded up, but I can see many a figure inside, laughing, joking, and singing with one another.

I take in a deep breath to brace myself, ,then try to enter as casually as I can. The last thing I wish is to end up in a brawl. I open the door and am taken aback by the loudness of the room. On the right, a group of men crowd around a table, playing cards.

One man has an eye stitched shut and a pipe poking out of his mouth. He is deep in concentration, his face full of thick grey hair that overcompensates for the lack of hair on his head. His one good eye shifts from his cards and lands on me, as if he is weighing up this stranger who has entered the tavern.

It has been some months since I was last in a tavern, and as much as I do like the atmosphere, the smell of stale smoke leaves something to be desired. The repugnant smell clings to me like an unwanted advance from a lady of the night. Heading towards the bar, I skirt around a man and a woman who are quarrelling. The woman wears a turquoise dress that kicks out as it hits her hips.

"You owe me another silver coin," she snarls at the man.

"Do we have a problem here?" A burley man wades over and stands beside the woman, crossing his arms. His dark, scarred skin is visible behind the thin, strapped braces that he wears to keep his pants aloft. The man stands at about six foot five and looks as though he could snap the scrawny man like a dry branch.

"No, no, not at all." The scrawny man fumbles around in his pocket and offers further coin to the woman he has underpaid.

She snatches it from him venomously. "What about the inconvenience?"

The man searches for another coin and passes it to her before the large man has an excuse to break his bones. "H-here, take this, sorry." Then he skulks away.

It takes a cowardly man to take something that does not belong to him, or not pay what is agreed upon.

"Can I help you?" the young woman behind the bar asks, jarring me from my entrancement.

She is an attractive woman with long, wavy blond hair, and when she flashes me a smile, I am pleasantly surprised that her teeth all remain. That is rare in these parts indeed.

"I'll take a pint of your strongest ale, please." Heavens, I need a drink after the skeletons we faced earlier.

"Ooh he's got manners as well as looks," she flirts with me. Though I know she probably takes this approach with all the men and women that enter here, I can't help but muster a coy smile.

"No need to be shy around me, I can help you with that too, if you know what I mean. But it will cost you a few more coin." The woman casts me cheeky wink, and I feel like a prized fish caught in a net.

"As much as I would like your company," I reply, not wanting to offend her, "I have pressing matters. I need to gather a crew for a voyage."

"And he's got his own ship, too! You, sir, are too good to be true. It's not very often we get a full house here, but you are a full house indeed, ain't ya?" She finishes pouring my ale and passes me a tankard that is as heavy as it is satisfying. The woman holds out her hand and waits for coin.

"Here." I pass her a silver piece, then bring the ale to my lips. I gulp it down as though I have been in the desert for the last week. The ale is dark and bitter, and the taste explodes in my mouth, the ruby notes souring my cheeks. After drinking it in one, I slam my tankard onto the bar and breathe a sigh of relief. That drink has been a long time coming.

The barmaid promptly refills my tankard. I take it and turn to survey the room. The game of cards looks like it is beginning to get heated as one disgruntled player slams his cards onto the table. He wears some form of plate armour that seems out of place for these parts. I can see some yellow markings, but from this angle it is difficult for me to see where his armour hails from. The ale has got the better of him. He loses his temper, and by the looks of it, the last of his coin.

"One more hand, Darmour," he whines, slurring his words. If he plays cards anything like he drinks, it is no wonder he lost.

"Ye've have had enough, Orjan," the one-eyed man advises. "I think it's time you leave." His gruff voice commands attention as he addresses the drunken player.

"At least give me a chance to win my coin back!" Orjan whimpers, slamming his hand onto the table which causes two drinks to spill.

The room falls silent and all eyes switch to the commotion that is building around the card table.

"Orjan, I suggest ye leave, lest ye really want to try my patience," Darmour growls.

"Maybe I should just take my coin back then," Orjan slurs, knocking the table again as he leans forward clumsily to retrieve his lost coin.

Darmour's chair screeches backwards. "Or maybe I can remove yer hand?" He stabs a dagger into the table, only just missing Orjan's fingers.

Orjan does not take kindly to this, and although most likely feeling more confident because of the rum he has been sinking, he is in no state to fight.

"You think it's okay to treat a knight in this manner?" he challenges, and I see his hands balling into fists as his cheeks redden with rage.

"I don't see no knight here, do ye, lads?" Darmour looks around him to the others at the card table, who shake their heads. They crack their knuckles and necks, readying for a bar brawl.

This is the last thing I wanted, and I pray that everyone will calm.

The room is charged as the group of men stare at Orjan, waiting for him to make a move. Orjan pulls his arm back as if he is going to swing a punch at someone. Sensing my opportunity, I step in and grab Orjan by the wrist, trying to stop the fallen knight from doing something he will later regret. There is tension in his arm as he struggles to free himself, confused.

"These kind gentlemen have asked you to leave, knight. I suggest you heed their advice before this matter escalates further." I speak calmly, yet my grip around his wrist is firm enough to let him know that I mean every word.

Orjan turns his head towards me. His gaunt face and overgrown beard tell me his troubles run far deeper than this game of cards.

"Let go of me," he growls. His breath smells of stale rum. The tension in his arm grows as he slowly tries to draw his arm free.

"I wish to see no harm brought to you," I tell him.

"Do not mistake me for someone who requires your charity," he snarls at me.

"Would ye look at that," Darmour interrupts, a wry smile forming in the corner of his mouth. "Looks like these two are havin' a lover's tiff."

Laughter erupts around the room.

I do not know what I expected when I tried to interject, and now I regret my actions, wishing that I was still enjoying my ale.

Riled by the laughter at his expense, Orjan pulls against my grip and his arm breaks free. He grabs his tankard and aims to strike me with it. I block the blow, but he loses his grip, sending the tankard flying across the room. It sprays its contents over a few people who have taken up watch, then bounces off the head of the burly man who came to the aid of the lady when I first arrived.

The giant of a man touches his head, then examines the blood on his fingers from the wound.

Like a bull, he charges at the two of us. I step to move out of the way but his speed is deceiving, and he catches me in the stomach, lifting me clean off my feet. Our momentum is only stopped by the table behind me, which cracks underneath our weight before it breaks in two. I feel the wind escape me from the force and I gasp for breath that does not come.

The room erupts into chaos as some of the men around the table are sent sprawling. Orjan begins throwing punches at anybody and everybody who stands too close to him. I am sure I see a tooth fly through the air.

The man on top of me seeks to stand and I push him up off me before I suffocate from the sheer weight of him. I plant my feet against his chest and push him back as hard as I can, sending him bounding into the side of Orjan. Orjan jumps out of the way, then leaps onto the giant's back and strikes him in the back of the head with ferocious speed.

The big man tries to shake him, moving backwards through the crowd until he hits the bar, sending Orjan crashing over the top. Glasses and drinks rain down on everyone as the barmaid screams in anger. Orjan's head pops up from behind the bar, but the barmaid stands over him with an empty bottle of rum clasped in her hand. She brings the bottle down on Orjan's head, who slumps and disappears back behind the bar.

"Get him out of here!" she screams. "Anyone else

wanting to end up like him and on the street?" She addresses the room like a commander, baring her teeth. "Get this bar cleaned up or you can all get out!"

All the men and women in the room instantly begin scuttling around, tidying up the mess like a well-rehearsed crew. It is clear to me that this is not the first time this has happened, nor would it be the last. I groan loudly as I sit myself up, the card game now ruined and underneath where I sit.

A rough hand greets me, and my gaze follows it to Darmour's grinning face.

"My advice when it comes to Orjan?" he says, taking my hand. "Don't get involved. He's not worth pig's piss." He helps me to my feet.

"I sought only to stop a brawl breaking out, one which would see him heavily outnumbered," I explain, rubbing the back of my head, which smarts from dropping through the table.

"Aye, fine job ye did there." Darmour laughs loudly and opens his arm out to allow me to survey the chaos that I have triggered. "We would have just thrown him out, like usual."

"It didn't look that way."

"And that is precisely the point, Mr. . . . ?"

"Ulrik."

"Ulrik, strong name that. As I was saying, my men and I know how to fight. We also know how to pick our battles. After all, what use are my men if they're dead?" Darmour chortles to himself. "We've been here long enough to realise that if you look menacing and act menacing, trouble tends to stay away. Well, except him. He keeps coming back wanting to play more cards. Threatening to expose us if we don't give him a chance to win his coin back. The man is a waste of skin and bone, and brings dishonour to whatever kingdom he hails from."

With this, two of Darmour's men help Orjan up and drag his unconscious body towards the front door, his legs trailing loosely behind him.

"What brings ye here, Ulrik? I ain't seen ye here before, and it isn't often people step in to help people they don't know."

"As it happens, I am searching for a crew," I begin. "I am hoping I have found just the men for the job." If this man is true to his word and behaves in a manner to avoid violence then maybe, just maybe, they are the men I need to help us run our stolen ship.

"In that case, we best discuss terms over a drink. Rita, a bottle of rum if ye would," he calls over to the barmaid, who smiles before stepping over the broken glass to fetch us the spirit.

Now I just have to hope these pirates will be more interested in finding the fountain of youth than turning me in for a handsome reward from the king, and that the contents of the fountain will free Esara of her burden, of the magic that courses through her.

# 24

## ZERINA

My arms feel as though I have bathed them in hot coals. I pour cold water over them to see if it helps, but it only makes the pain worse, and tears stream down my face. This is the worst I have ever felt after magic use, but I did summon more power than ever before.

The feeling of euphoria is a distant memory. A tremble has overcome me, and as much as my arms burn, the rest of me feels freezing. I try to pick up a cup filled with water but by the time I bring it to my lips, there is hardly any water remaining. I take a sip and aim to place the cup back on the table to my side, but I drop it when the bottom clips the edge of the table. With a crash, the cup shatters into pieces, and I let out a scream of frustration. I cannot cope with this pain much longer.

I curse myself for succumbing to the temptation to use magic again. Maybe if we had held out that little bit longer, we would have found a way. Then again, we might all be dead in that cave, bound to defend its grounds like the skeletal warriors.

In the heat of the fight, my instincts had taken over. It felt like my mind and my body knew exactly what to do, like the magic took control of me and knew how to keep us safe. I merely had to let it in, let it flow through my body, a conduit like metal is to heat.

With this pain, I don't understand how anyone would want to summon such dark forces. Still, Esara and Ulrik are safe, and we have the drawing and our next destination, just like Lyrissa wanted.

My arms feel as if they are made of stone. Each time I move them, daggers drag through my flesh. When I try to relax, the palms of my hands cramp with intense pain, causing my fingers to coil in on themselves, forcing hardened fists. I embed my nails into my skin, and blood begins to force its way through the cracks of my fingers.

Unable to cope, I fall from my chair and begin convulsing uncontrollably, screaming out in perpetual agony. If this is to be my fate, then I wish that death had swallowed me up like ship in a maelstrom.

Minutes feel like hours as I writhe around on the floor like a snake, uncontrolled and wild. The floorboards splinter into my bare legs, each one causing me to wince and convulse more. All I wish for in this moment is a release from this torture, a way to make it stop.

I feel the pull in my stomach first, then a slight spike in my adrenaline. I do not know if I am in control or not. The darkness of the room is slowly illuminated by my hands which begin to glow softly. Instantly, the burning sensation dampens, and a warm, soothing sensation pulsates through my arms up to my elbows.

I am able to uncoil the tight fists that had been forced upon me. Blood lines my fingertips, and I can see the line of broken skin in my palms but even that does not cause me pain now. Magic runs through me once more, just enough to alleviate the pain. The discomfort does not fully leave me, but at least now I can tolerate it.

My head becomes awash with an imbalance that causes the room to feel slightly amiss, as if I drank too much ale or even ate some poisonous shrooms. I am unsteady on my feet, and I stumble into the table which catches me from falling over again. It is a strange feeling, but it draws me to the euphoric feeling I felt in the cave.

I want to start dancing. I try to focus on my outstretched hands, but all I see are blurred forms where they should be. I fall face first onto my bed, the bedding feeling angelically soft against my skin. My senses feel a hundred times stronger than they usually do. The room dances around me, and my bed begins rocking back and forth as if I am being cradled to sleep by my mother.

At last, I can sleep.

# 25

## ZERINA

'The sanded plains of Karapeah is the home of the fabled falls of Rahuka. Water so fresh that is able to cure the hardest of ailments. Stories have passed down from family to family in the local regions. No one however knows its true location. Such a tonic would be more valuable than the wars that it could create.'

Entry from 'The Lost Treasures Of The World' - 243 KR

The light beams through the gap in my curtains, warming my toes where it lands. I reluctantly open my eyes, feeling as though I have spent a night drinking ale. My head throbs as I sit up in bed, but apart from the odd ache over my body, I feel surprisingly okay. The affliction from over-using my magic seems to have passed.

I pull myself from my bed and adjust my night gown, moving to the windows to let in more light. When I pull the curtains to the side, I am overcome with the bright sun, and it takes a moment for my eyes to adjust from the darkness in the room. Given how high the sun is, it must be nearing midday.

I dress myself, tying my hair, and pour myself some water to aid my dry mouth, then I hastily tuck my blouse into my pants. Esara's room is just a few doors down, and I knock lightly before entering to see if she is there.

"Esara?" I speak tentatively. She is not here, but her bedding lies at the base of her bed, and it is clear she sleeps like a wildling. Her room is in a state, but it is not for me to encourage her to clean up.

Ulrik's room sits at the end of the corridor. It is the smallest out of the three that he paid for, something that he had insisted on.

When I reach the entrance to his room, I tap lightly against the wooden door, not wishing to startle the two of them should they be in there.

"Yes?" Ulrik responds groggily.

I push open the door. "Have you seen Esa – " the sight before me cuts my words short. Ulrik lies in his bed with only a sheet covering his modesty. My eyes are drawn to the muscles that decorate his front and the scars that trace his body. Then my gaze lands on the naked woman that lies beside him. She does not have the privilege of a sheet to cover her.

Unfazed by my arrival, she smiles at me before sitting up and dropping her long blond hair over her shoulder.

"Zerina!" Ulrik bolts up from the bed and grabs the sheets to cover his manhood. "I, erm . . ." He looks around his room, searching for his clothes.

"I'm sorry!" I spin on my heels so that I do not see any more. I have already seen too much. "I am looking for Esara, I thought she might be with you." I feel my cheeks burn scarlet, and I wish I could sink through the floor.

"Zerina, please, I can explain – "

"Ulrik, I do not require an explanation. You have needs that you must express, like all other men."

"Zerina, please," Ulrik calls out, but I am already shuffling down the corridor as quickly as possible. I have no idea what I was expecting, walking into his room like that, but seeing him naked with another woman was not it.

I head to the beach, surprised by the emotions that I am feeling. I have only just met the man, and I have no rights to command who he lies with.

But part of me wishes it was me.

I banish the thought. I am a foolish girl, inexperienced with men, and I have been naive to grow in my affections towards Ulrik. After all, I have only known the man for a week. Clearly Ulrik likes the company of much more experienced women.

My thoughts turn venomously towards the woman in his bed. But this is not me, this is not the woman I am.

I reach the exit of the inn and am grateful to be greeted by the fresh breeze.

"Zerina, you're awake!" Esara exclaims when she sees me. She sits poking a crab with a stick. The disgruntled crab raises its claws in an attempt to remove her weapon from her. Her smile is exactly what I need right now, and it brings me enough reassurance to centre my thoughts and gather myself.

I smile at her as she leaves the poor crab alone and approaches me.

"How are you feeling?" she asks, wrapping her arms around me. The warmth of her hug is as if she has not seen me for months. "I could hear you crying in your room last night, it scared me. I was really worried about you." She squeezes me even tighter, and my heart melts at the affection.

"I am okay. Unfortunately it is a side effect of the magic. I feel much better this morning," I try to reassure her. It must have been terrifying for a girl of her age to hear such wailing coming from my room. I place my arms around her and squeeze her back. "Thank you," I tell her.

"Do you know if my brother is up yet? The cheek of him to tell me to get a good night's rest, when he has slept in until nearly dinner time!"

Esara is too young to understand that her brother has not been doing any sleeping last night. "Erm, he should be with us soon enough," I tell her.

"I bet he had one too many drinks. He was meant to be searching for a crew to help us with our quest."

"Go easy on him, Esara, your brother carries a lot of stress. He needs to be able to blow off some steam." My thoughts return to him in his room with that woman and I feel another pang of jealously. Something I need to learn to deal with very quickly.

# 26
## ULRIK

My head pounds, and the taste of stale rum clings to the inside of my mouth like an unwanted plague.

I search for my boots so that I can go find Zerina and Esara, knowing full well just how awkward a conversation will be right now.

"You in a hurry?" Rita ruffles behind me, padding around like a cat. On another day and if still in the King's Navy, I would dive back into bed and spend as long as possible with the pleasurable company, though my memory of our time together last night is foggy at best. I do not recall what time we returned to my room. Darmour and I were well into our second bottle of rum before it was chucking out time at the inn.

Zerina's face was a picture of disappointment when she saw us, and although I know I have nothing to feel sorry for, guilt washes over me and I do not know why.

"We need to begin repairs on our ship if we are to set sail in a timely manner. I need to find my crew," I explain.

"Shame, would have liked to spend a few more hours

with you. You are a dark horse ain't ya?" She kneels up on the bed and gives me a kiss on the cheek, then dons her dress. She puts on her boots and heads to the door before turning. "Make sure you come pay me a visit next time you're in Voraz. There's not enough men like you, Ulrik." And with that she leaves my room.

Deciding not to make things more awkward by leaving together, I opt to wait another ten minutes before heading down to the beach.

The heat of the sun beats down on me and I regret putting on my jacket; it absorbs the heat like a sponge.

"Took your time, lazy bones," Esara teases, waving me to join her and Zerina in the sand. Zerina appears to be in good spirits, and she doesn't look as though she is bothered by what she has seen. Maybe the best step forward is to not make a big deal out of this. After all, I am a man, one with needs. I have committed no crime.

I walk up confidently to the two of them. "Good morning, ladies."

"Say, for it's not morning, dear brother." Esara laughs. "How can you sleep in so late on a day like today?"

She is too young to understand the inner workings of men, and for that I am grateful. She is still an innocent girl, despite the horrors she has already witnessed. "Did I not deserve such a lie in after yesterday's exploits? It is not every day that you do battle with a band of skeletons." I pause for a moment. "Or assemble a crew for a ship."

Esara beams, and she begins jumping and cheering at my news. She dives at me and wraps her arms around me, showing me her pride. It is moments like this I wish I could cherish forever. All I need is to know that she is safe and happy. Today I know she is both, but whether that will remain is a question I do not have the answer to.

"When do we meet them?" Esara asks.

"We best head to the ship now." I ruffle Esara's head playfully as she tries to fight me off. "Zerina, you look well this morning." I try to hide my surprise. The last time she used magic, it took her two days to rid herself of her affliction. Yesterday she used far more magic than before, and today she seems as though she has already recovered.

"I am grateful to have woken up in far less pain than I was in last night," she replies without making eye contact. "And if you please, I do not wish to talk about it."

Respecting her wishes, I decide not to press her on the matter, although she seems off with me from this morning. I cannot help but wonder if she is concealing her pain.

In Voraz, the market is far busier than when I came here yesterday. There was rain last night, and vendors splash through the mud, trading food, spices, and fruit. The weaponsmith from yesterday notices me, casting me a toothless smile which sends a shiver down my spine. We pass a group of men outside The Two Shovels, which is the cause of my headache. They throw me a wave as we walk by.

Our ship sits on the far side of the harbour. It is in a sorry state compared to the others that line the docks. The sails have seen better days, and the hull could probably do with some attention, but for now it is all we have.

Seeing the ship bob in the ocean causes a wave of nausea to wash over me, and I begin to regret last night's rum, suppressing the urge to vomit.

When we reach the ship, the sound of laughter from a group that stand just beyond it catches my attention. It is

Darmour with his crew. Despite us getting into a drunken mess, he has stayed true to his word.

"Fine day for setting sail, captain," Darmour addresses me as we reach them. He takes a deep breath as if savouring the smell of the fresh sea air.

"Oi! Why are you presuming my brother is the captain?" Esara scolds Darmour seriously, dressing him down.

"Ye must be Esara, you are exactly as your brother told me." Darmour smiles as he kneels in front of her, submitting to her command.

Esara seems pleased with this, and her smile magnifies. "You may stand, sir."

Darmour gives her an exaggerated bow before his attention switches to Zerina. "And you must be Zerina." He takes her hand and raises it, kissing it lightly. "Ulrik did not tell me of your beauty."

I cannot help but notice Zerina's blushing cheeks. Despite Darmour being twice her age, the man is full of confidence and charm.

I clear my throat. "Esara, Zerina. This is Darmour."

"May I introduce ye to some of my crew?" Darmour points to the group behind him who instantly fall into line.

He leads us down the line, introducing them one at a time. First up is a strange looking fellow who is tall and gangly, with skin cracked like dried dirt. His hair is slicked back, and when I look him over, I see that in one of his hands, his fingers are coiled uncomfortably. It is a sign of creken finger, a nasty disease that has a tendency to deform the digits of those unfortunate enough to catch it.

"His names Tobias," Darmour says. "Spent his whole adult life at sea and is a fine sailor who I would trust with my life."

"Glad to hear it." I nod with approval.

"Pleasure to meet your acquaintance," Zerina follows up with a little curtsy.

"This is Doran." Darmour points out the bouncer from The Two Shovels who was responsible for dropping me through the table. His frame is even bigger than I remember, his dark shin shining in the sunlight.

I laugh. "We are already acquainted." It will prove us in good stead to have such a man on our ship.

"This here is Navi, she's good in the shadows, one of the best pickpockets in Voraz." A short, scrawny woman with catlike amber eyes stands next in line, her hair hidden under a bandana. "Helpful for pilfering coin of unsuspecting folk if we have to make port somewhere."

Next up are two men of average build, both with short, dirty blond hair. Their similarities are remarkable. The only difference I notice is that one has blue eyes and the other has brown. They both appear dishevelled in dirty, torn clothes that are far too small for them.

"Luko and Marik. These two are unable to speak in our tongue, but they follow instructions, and I can assure you they are good fighters. No idea how they landed here. Luko is the one with blue eyes, Marik, brown."

"And finally, this is Yigress, as fierce as the ocean." Yigress is the biggest woman that I have ever set eyes on, a good foot taller than me. Her head is shaved, and she has nasty-looking scars on her face. I can't help but stare. The scarred lines look as though she scribed them into her own skin.

Yigress salutes me. "The pleasure's mine." Her voice is deep but assured.

"The lines on her face are how she keeps tally of the men she has killed. She tells me this is what the people of her tribe do. If ye ask me, it's such a dreadful shame for what would be a fine face." Darmour speaks to me as if Yigress and the other members of the crew are not standing there. "She is a woman not to be messed with," he warns.

Esara stares at the tall woman with fascination.

"This is it then, this is yer crew," Darmour announces.

"What do you mean my crew? Are these not your people?" I ask.

"I thought ye were a seaman. Have ye no idea how this whole piracy game works? Have ye forgotten our conversations last night already?" Darmour bursts into laughter, as does the rest of the crew. "Shut yer faces," he commands. They stop laughing immediately. "Show yer captain some respect."

He turns to face me before continuing, "We have agreed terms to having me and my crew aid ye, fifty-five percent of anything we find, forty-five to you." He offers his hand to shake and cement the deal.

I shake his hand firmly. I am not a greedy man, and the deal seems fair given the aid this crew will give us on our voyage. "We have a deal, Darmour." I smile, grateful our paths crossed.

"Now that we have an agreement, might ye tell us where it is we be heading?"

I remove the drawing from the inside of my jacket. "Treventine," I tell him.

"That's a long voyage that ye have planned for us. Tell me, what is it ye seek on the barren island of Treventine?"

I smile and unfurl the cloth drawing from the cave. "We are searching for this. We are heading for the fountain of youth."

# 27

## ZERINA

*'The sea does not take pity on those who cross her. Her power and might unmatched by any other natural force in the worlds.'*
*Saduka Herald - 255 KR*

With the help of Darmour and the others, the necessary repairs have been made to the ship. Ulrik refused to set sail until it was safe to do so. The fact that all these people are about to embark on a voyage that all began because of a vision I had weighs heavily on my mind.

It has been two weeks since meeting the crew. Darmour has a look of the man still sceptical about our destination, yet he commits to the voyage all the same. He is an intriguing man, confident in the way he talks, and he has a swagger about him that I am surprised to find pleasing. He is older than Ulrik by fifteen or twenty years, and despite his face bearing the weathered skin of a man who has traversed the sea all his life, I do find him good looking.

The rest of the crew have set about loading the ship,

readying for us to set sail. The two foreign twins, Luko and Marik, carry crates of vegetables across the platform, and Navi sits in the crow's nest, pulling up rope. The others are out of sight as they set about the ship, completing the tasks they have been instructed to do by Darmour.

There is an electricity about us in our excitement to depart, and it is a distraction I welcome; my hands still tremble from the magic use, but I am able to hide this from the others. The new crew cannot see me as weak and unable to help.

At the front of the ship, Yigress shows Esara a move to defend herself with, and Esara copies the woman, dagger in hand. All I can think is sorrow for the man that would find himself on the receiving end of the strike.

"Zerina," Ulrik waves his hand to summon me over to him and Darmour, and I take the wooden steps slowly, not wishing to lose my balance. We may be in shallow waters, but the ship still rocks gently with the tide, causing me to concentrate in order to navigate the steps down from the ship's wheel.

"Zerina, you, Esara and I will be bunking in the captain's chambers. I have explained to Darmour that I would sleep below deck with the rest of the crew, but he will not have it," Ulrik tells me. He had no issue with sharing the captain's quarters with us on our way here, so I find it strange that suddenly he is offering to sleep below deck. This must be down to what happened with the woman I found him in the company of. Perhaps he is feeling as awkward about the situation as I am.

Darmour raises his eyebrows in a sceptical manner, which causes me to smile. "I was explaining to Ulrik that he is the captain of this ship, and as such, he needs to stay in the captain's quarters. It will send the wrong message to the crew otherwise. They respond best to command. You know, to hierarchy." He winks at me playfully and I feel my cheeks turn scarlet with a rush of blood.

"May I ask what the command is, if Ulrik is captain?" I cannot let these two think that as men they automatically get to take charge of the ship and of the crew. I have more than proven myself with my magic, but the new crew does not know that.

"Well, erm, we was thinking as Ulrik is captain that it would be best if I was his first mate on this voyage, miss," Darmour mumbles, fumbling for his words. I can't help but find his discomfort entertaining. "I know this crew and they trust me. They do not know ye so as yet there is no trust from them."

I face Ulrik who looks in as much discomfort as Darmour, and nod my head towards him. "I will be in the quarters, captain." I let the word roll playfully off my tongue as I turn to leave. The muscles in my cheeks ache as I try my hardest to suppress my smile, something I fail miserably at. It is not often that I am confident enough to challenge men with sass, but it is something I could get used to if it makes me feel this good about myself.

"Let me on the ship, dammit!" someone tells from the gangway. Curious, I move to the side of the ship and peer over to see where the commotion is coming from. Doran stands with his arms outstretched, refusing to let a dishevelled man climb aboard.

The man is unkempt. He wears yellow plated armour, although sections of it appear to be missing or rusted. He has a broken shield strapped to his back, and a weapon I have never seen before fastened to his waist. His face is drawn; the man looks exhausted and, if I am not mistaken, a little drunk.

"I said leave, Orjan. I have no time for this. You are like a fly that I cannot swat," says, Doran, pushing the man backwards.

Orjan stumbles, clearly not just from Doran's shove.

"Piss, it's that drunkard," Darmour curses as he looks over the side with me. "Didn't think he would be up by now! He's been after a way off this island for weeks now."

"You know this man?" I ask.

"I can't get rid of him, he's like a bad smell." Darmour leans over the side of the boat, a wild grin on his face. 'Take yerself off, maybe try havin' a bath!"

Orjan's gaze splays upwards as he searches for where the voice came from, all the while struggling to remain on his feet. "Darmour," he calls up, "Darmour, please!" His voice breaks.

I glance at Darmour, who merely appears entertained.

Orjan drops to his knees. "Please, I just need passage off this island, I need to find a way home." He brings his hands up to his face and sobs into them.

He is broken, and it is heart-breaking to see. Whatever this man has done, he does not deserve this embarrassment.

"Let him aboard," I call down to Doran, who spins to look at me in disbelief before looking at Darmour. "I said let him aboard!" There is a sternness to my voice that even I am shocked by.

"Miss, if I may advise against this," Darmour starts, but I am not interested in his words.

"The man is clearly desperate and in need of help. I do not see what harm it can do, letting him on board and granting him safe passage."

Darmour turns to Ulrik who simply shrugs at him. "It is

not only my wishes that need to be listened to on this voyage. If she says let him aboard, then let him aboard."

"Aye, captain. Let the pig aboard," Darmour commands.

Doran steps to the side and Orjan makes his way up the walkway towards the main deck of the ship where we stand.

When he reaches me, he almost loses his footing entirely and stumbles in my direction.

"Thank you, madam," he says. I can smell the ale on his breath, but I am determined not to regret my decision. "My name is Orjan, knight of Rashouya."

I feel sceptical about his title, given his current state. "Well, Orjan, knight of Rashouya, if you are to seek passage on this ship there are a few rules you must abide by," I begin. "First of all, you are to go below deck and sleep off whatever toxins you have in your body. Second of all, you will not touch anything that will cause you to behave in the manner that you greet me in."

"Anything else, madam?" Orjan feigns a bow and I contemplate pushing him overboard myself and saving the crew the job.

"Yes, three, get a bloody wash. Go now, before I change my mind." My assertiveness seems enough to get him moving, and Orjan bows properly before staggering away. Within a few moments he is gone from sight and his stench slowly fades. Around me, the crew scowls. I hope I do not live to regret my decision.

# 28

## ULRIK

"It's one thing to set sail on a ship without a name, but to bring him aboard, captain!" Darmour is restless and frustrated, and we have only just set off.

"I understand your concerns about the knight, but Zerina has offered to watch over him and make sure he doesn't cause us any trouble," I try to reassure him, but in all honesty, naming the ship is not something that has even crossed my mind. Some consider it bad luck to set sail on a ship that has no name. It is something we must give thought to, as it is not only Darmour who grows restless on our maiden voyage.

The crew are not best pleased. The ship feels steady for the time, and I stand to the rear, gripping the wheel tightly as we remain true on our course. Darmour has calculated that it may take as long as three months to get to Treventine, with some treacherous waters to traverse along the way. For now, I enjoy the relative calm that we find ourselves in, the only semblance of a storm coming from my new first mate Darmour.

There is a steady breeze that feels refreshing to the skin, and the gulls stalk the boat, a sign that we are still close to the shoreline. Navi sits in the crow's nest keeping watch, and Luko, Marik, and Doran are busy swabbing the deck. Tobias and Yigress fool around with Esara, continuing to show her tricks for her to learn with her dagger. Esara seems happy enough, her youthful mind not able to comprehend the dangers we will face out at sea. Even that is better than the fate that awaits if the king's men get their hands on her.

I watch intently as Esara breaks from her training with her new mentors to take a drink from her flask. Little does she know that the tasteless remedy our mother taught me is mixed into her drink. It is the only way that I can keep the magic buried within her. The last thing I want now is for Esara to succumb to the side effects of wielding her suppressed powers. When she is old enough, I am sure she will understand.

"It's a fine day for sailing, captain," Darmour says, dragging me from my thoughts like a winch. "With that map and a good wind behind us, I feel that the gods may be on our side. Once we meet Treventine, we'll know whether we're on a wild reevit chase, or if the fountain of youth really does exist."

I look out at the huge expanse of water, the island of Voraz a mere memory behind us. The scope of how tiny we are in comparison to the waters is apparent.

"Let's hope I have not cast us all out on a fool's treasure hunt," I reply.

Darmour seems to pick up on my anxieties.

"Yer doin' a grand job, captain," Darmour reassures me. "Keep the crew onside, reward them well, and they will run through the fires of hell for you." He turns to face the open water and breathes in a huge gulp of air like a wine connoisseur savouring every note.

"For too long have I spent my time in Voraz," he continues. "Don't get me wrong, Voraz has been kind to me, but I've missed this. The sway of a ship and the spray of the ocean, the hollerin' of good men and women happy with their duties."

"Where did you serve?" I am sure that like myself, Darmour has spent time in the King's Fleet.

Hesitantly, he responds, "I was in the merchant navy for nearly twenty years. Twenty years that shaped me into the man I am today." His eyes become distant as he stares back out to sea. "It was my greatest honour to serve the king in his crusades, protecting ships that carried much needed cargo to the king's armies. Some of the best years of my life but also some of the worst. The things I have seen, the things I have witnessed out there, it would reduce any man to a quivering mess." He squeezes the side of the ship with his planted hands and breathes in another wave of fresh, salted air.

"What happened?"

Darmour casts a wry look over his shoulder. "That, captain, is a tale for another day." He gives me a false smile as he turns to walk towards the crew.

"When I have earned your trust?" I call out behind him, curious to the life behind the man who has agreed to help us.

"Aye, captain."

Stepping to the side of the boat, I take a moment to take in the open sea and gather my own thoughts. It seems that no matter how hard I try, I am destined to be out on the open water. From experience, I know I'll manage the journey just fine, but I worry how Esara and

Zerina will cope once we hit the rough waters of Yugo's Tears.

Beside the ship, a group of halindras splash as they follow us. The sea creatures are a playful sort, and their presence is a good omen. A green crust coats their slimline bodies, shining like emeralds in the sun. Halindras are a rare creature to see, and are often hunted for their highly valued skins. I count three larger halindras and four smaller ones, their pointed faces coming into view as they launch themselves out of the water one at a time, as if taking it in turn to see who can jump the highest. It brings a smile to my face.

"Ship ahoy!" Navi's shrill voice calls down from the crow's nest where she perches. She grips a spyglass in her hands, searching over the waters to the rear of our ship.

I climb the steps to the quarterdeck, my heart jumping. I reach for my own spyglass, fearing that it is a naval ship on our tail.

It takes a few moments for me to find the ship, and when I do, it is like nothing I have ever seen. The ship is larger than ours, giving us the advantage of speed should we need it. The body of the ship is a pale oak colour, a wood I have never seen used before which piques out my curiosity. The flags are hoisted, with light blue colours and a strange symbol etched onto them that I am not familiar with. The ship seems to be moving at a slower pace than we are, but it points in our direction.

"What is it, captain?" Darmour asks.

I pass him my spyglass, which he brings up to his face with anticipation. Like myself, it takes a few moments for him to see what Navi has alerted us to.

"It can't be," he starts. "It's Elvish."

That cannot be right.

"Darmour, there have not been Elvish ships in these waters for hundreds of years. How is it that you make such wild claims?"

When Darmour lowers the spyglass, there is panic in his eyes in place of his usual confidence. "I ain't a well-read man, but even I can recognise the symbol they hoist on their flag."

He forces his hand into my inside pocket, removes the detailed drawing from the cave, and slaps it against my chest. "See for yourself," he commands.

I unfurl the drawing of the chalice and I realise that Darmour is correct in his deductions. In the corner of the drawing, in the same style as the ship's flags, sits a faded Elvish symbol: an outline of a tree under a circle with a 'v' on top. I grab the spyglass from Darmour and search for the ship once more, confirming Darmour's theory. The symbol matches that which is on the cloth drawing.

"I do not believe in coincidences, captain."

"Nor do I Darmour, nor do I." They move at a slower pace than us, as if they are following us.

"What's going on?" Zerina voice arrives from behind, startling us both.

"We are being followed by an Elvish ship," Darmour explains.

"What does that mean?" she asks, an air of concern coming over her. "Do they mean to harm us?"

"Look." I wave the cloth in front of her. She looks down at it, then back up at the ship.

"Here miss, take a look for yourself." Darmour points to the spyglass in my hand, and I pass it to her.

Zerina searches the waters for those that seem to follow us. After a short while, she lets out a sigh of frustration. "I don't see anything."

"Keep searching, miss, you will see it. You just need to get used to using a spyglass on a moving ship." Darmour moves behind her and holds her arms steady. "Do you see it now?" A pang of jealousy hits me in the chest and catches me off guard.

"No, maybe I am doing it wrong?" She passes the spyglass back to Darmour who inquisitively raises it to search for the ship once more. Then he lowers the tool, a puzzled expression painted over him. "It's gone."

"What do you mean it's gone?" I demand. "Ships don't just disappear."

"I am telling you, captain, the ship has gone." Darmour looks just as confused as I feel.

This is not a good sign.

We are being followed by an Elvish ship linked to the elixir that we seek to find. The fact that the ship has vanished concerns me more than anything.

All we can do is stay vigilant as we continue our journey to Treventine.

# 29

## ZERINA

'Eight coins, with no purpose or power between them when separated, but entirely different when together. It is thought that even the gods feared the magic that these pieces of eight possess. It is for this reason that they spread them across the world. So that they became forgotten, a distant story told by pirates and buccaneers. Little do they know that they exist, I have two of them. You need to meet me, you need to hear about what I have seen. These coins can help, they can grant a power like non seen before in this world.'

*Letter to Morgana from anonymous - 263 KR*

"Are you ok?" Esara sits up in her bed to check on my welfare.

With laboured breathing, I prise myself away from the feeling of nausea that I have been suppressing for the last two hours.

We have been at sea for over a week now, and just as I was beginning to feel accustomed to life on a ship, the sea brings me down to earth like the crashing of a wave. The ship rocks gently, which does not sit well with me, and another tidal of hot flashes overcomes me. I reach for the jug at the side of my bed and pour myself some water, which I gulp down.

"Try not to drink too much," Esara says delicately. "The more that's in your belly, the more there is to come back up. Yigress told me." She beams at the nugget of wisdom that has been imparted to her.

"I'll be fine, I just need to get used to this life." It is strange living somewhere that is constantly on the move, constantly rocking, constantly creaking and groaning as if our home is alive, as if it speaks. A life where I must perfectly time each step I take with the rocking of the ship, a skill that I have yet to master.

The urge to exit the captain's quarters becomes too much, and I can feel the bile in my stomach forcing its way up, burning my throat.

"Are you – " Esara starts, but I jump from my bed and make my way to the door, almost removing it from its hinges as I exit.

The ice-cold breeze catches me off guard. I am not suitably dressed for being out here at this time, and goosebumps cover my arms in an instant. It is a welcome change from the unbearable hot flashes.

The main deck is eerily quiet, with only the waves to be heard. Seeing the boat sway as it moves through the waves is enough to finish me off. Leaning over the side of the boat, I heave uncontrollably, and what feels like everything inside of me exits. The burning sensation in my throat is the most difficult to tolerate, and to my despair, my dizziness does not subside even after vomiting.

The soft glow of a nearby torch illuminates my immediate surroundings, and above, Ulrik and Darmour stand at the ship's wheel. I flush with embarrassment, but they seem to feign conversation, as if to pretend they have not seen me succumbing to ocean sickness. It is a gesture I appreciate, but my cheeks continue to burn. Not only have they seen me spewing, but I am standing on the main deck with only a shirt to cover my modesty.

"Madam." Orjan's greeting startles me.

Now I can add Orjan to the list of men who have witnessed my embarrassing state.

"Orjan," I reply, not as assertively as I intend. "Can I help you?"

He sits on one of the barrels tied around the mast in the centre of the ship. Although I cannot see his face clearly, I recognise the rusted yellow armour that he wears. He raises something to his mouth, and with crunch, I can tell he is eating an apple. My mind is drawn back to the rotten one I ate with Esara, the thought of which almost causes me to heave once more.

"Just admiring the view," he says. My hackles rise. How dare he address me in such a way.

Although his strange accent is soft, his voice is rough like gravel. He takes another bite of his apple and stands. "You will get used to it, madam. I can assure you that the sickness gets easier."

"Must be easier when you are used to staggering around all the time," I snap, still annoyed by his comment. "Tell me, is this the longest you have gone without a drink?"

"In fact it is, yes. To be honest madam, I am disappointed that you would use my own affliction against me."

This sends a jolt through my body. Does Orjan know of my struggles with magic?

He moves closer, stepping into the torchlight, and it is clear by how he carries himself that he is sober. His long, dirty blond hair is slicked back, and thick, greying stubble fills his worn face, a face that is tired and drawn. His dark eyes, although more alert than the last time I saw him, sill seem somewhat vacant, as if Orjan is not truly here.

"I have no idea how long it has been. I have many a memory lost since way before I landed on the shores of Voraz," Orjan explains. "I have woken with many a scar, my body battered and bruised, with no recollection of how I came about them." He searches into the dark void surrounding the ship and breathes in the sea air.

There is a mutual silence between us, and to my surprise, it is not uncomfortable.

"Thank you," Orjan exhales as if the words are difficult to force from his mouth.

"What have I done?"

"You have given me means to escape the endless hell on that island. You have forced me to become that which I have not been for so long."

"What have you become?"

"Sober." He pauses. "I can tell you are new to this life, madam. You will learn that the world is a cruel place. Kindness is a gift. I could say it is rarer than the treasure that you now search for."

"You know not of the cruelness that I have faced, Orjan. Please do not let my inexperience of the world trick you into thinking I have not experienced it."

"I merely wished to offer my thanks. You offered me a chance when no other would."

As Orjan turns to leave, I feel a pang of guilt for snapping at him. "Perhaps you can tell me more when I am not in a state myself," I say, smiling towards him, but I am unsure if the darkness obscures my face.

Orjan casts a wave goodbye as he heads to the lower deck where the crew sleeps. Turning to face the darkness, I accept the cold wind that presses against my face, and it soothes me.

"How are you feeling?"

I jump as Ulrik appears by my side.

"I have never felt so sick in my life," I reply. It is a blatant lie; after the affliction caused by magic use, this sickness pales in comparison.

"Has Orjan offended you?" He brushes hair away from my face that is matted against my forehead, a combination of the wind and my own clammy skin.

I could not feel more unattractive in this state, and I pull my head away from him and brush my hair behind my ear. "Do you not think I am able to hold my own against a fallen knight? Have you forgotten already what we have been through in our short time together?" I attempt to sound playful, but I am uncertain it works.

Ulrik steps back, panicked in expression. "Apologies, Zerina. Now I am the one offending you."

I laugh at his response. "Ulrik, I wasn't being serious."

Ulrik relaxes and feigns a laugh himself, but I think this is more nervousness than anything.

A wave of heat pulses through me, and I know what is coming. Just as I can no longer hold back the renewed nausea, I lean over the side of the ship once more and wretch. When it's over, I stumble backwards, and I feel the firmness of Ulrik's arms as he steadies me as best he can.

"I've got you," he reassures me, scooping me up.

The dizziness makes it hard to see clearly, and I shut my

eyes, wrapping my arms tightly against Ulrik's neck. I bury my head into him, hoping the darkness will make the dizziness go away.

"Come, the best thing for you is sleep. You will feel better in the morning."

I pray that Ulrik's words ring true, because we still have at least a moon's cycle before we reach Treventine.

# 30
## ZERINA

"Stow the sails!" Darmour's voice cracks as he roars his commands at the crew. "Yugo's Tears will be our biggest test. These waters are treacherous on a calm day."

The clouds around us have turned dark, blocking out the sun as though it is the dead of night, even though it is the middle of the day.

"I do not like these clouds, Darmour." Ulrik searches the skies above us, his face gaunt with worry. He drops his gaze towards me. "Zerina, make sure Esara stays in my quarters."

"Come with me." I offer my hand to Esara who grips hold of it tightly. She staggers next to me when the ship rocks as we ride a large wave. Her confidence is replaced with the fear of a child. This is by far the roughest waters we have traversed so far. If not for my own worries, I could empty the contents of my stomach from the sickness that has consumed me. Not through magic use but through the violent rocking we have endured for the last hour. I have no idea what we need to do in this situation. Would it not be safer for the crew to remain below deck?

"Storm could dead ahead!" Navi's shrill voice reaches us as I open the door to the captain's quarters and guide Esara inside.

"Stay with me, please stay with me." Her panicked face tugs at my heart.

"Please stay in here, Esara, I must help the crew. If your brother tells me to return here then I will."

"I am scared, Zerina." Tears form in the corners of her eyes and I pull her towards me and squeeze. Esara's arms wrap around me.

"Fear can consume us if we allow it. It can affect the decisions we make. Turn that fear into courage. I need you to be brave, Esara. Can you do that for me?" I step back from her and Esara wipes her sleeve across her face. "We will be okay, Esara, we just need to get through these waters."

Darmour has been warning us about the waters in Yugo's Tears, but being in the moment, I feel that his words have not been harsh enough. I plant my foot behind me as the ship hits another wave and rocks backwards. The spray of water reaches me in the doorway of which I need to grab hold of to keep from sliding backwards. Esara stumbles into me, but I am able to keep us both in place until we eventually level out.

"I need you to get into bed. If you feel us rocking, grab hold of the bedpost." It is the only advice I can offer; I have never been in this position and have no idea where would be best for Esara to shelter.

Esara scurries to the bed and dives on top, where she keels up and casts me another panicked look.

I cast her a half smile and close the door, praying she will be okay inside.

"Zerina, lend us your hands." Orjan is pulling on a rope but it is slipping from his grip. I reach him at the same time as Yigress and the two of us grab hold of the rope and start pulling. The weight is incredible and I am surprised that Orjan was able to hold this position on his own. As we pull the rope, the lower sails tug upwards as if drawing on curtains. The rope burns against the soft skin on my palms, the ache in my arms becoming more noticeable.

"Can you two hold this position?" says Yigress, looking over her shoulder. Orjan casts her a nod and she lets go.

The pull catches me off guard and I am shunted forward, but I plant my feet. Orjan leans back, pulling with all his strength to keep the sail in place. I copy him and lean backwards, gripping the rope even tighter. It groans as it stretches but we are able to keep our position. Yigress climbs the lower part of the mast and begins to tie up sections of the sail. The ship continues to sway back and forth, making it increasingly difficult to hang on, but some- how, we manage it.

"Clear!" Yigress yells.

We slacken off the rope and Orjan heads towards the mast with the excess in his hands. I look up to see Yigress climbing farther up the mast, where she begins tying the rest of the larger sails that Marik, Luko, and Doran have stowed.

"Storm dead ahead!" Navi calls out.

"Brace yourselves!" Darmour shouts as if in the midst of battle.

A wave of rain reaches us, stinging my face as it bounces off my skin. I never knew rain could be so heavy, and it feels like I am being pelted with stones. No sooner does the rain hit us, the wind crashes into us and suddenly the deck of the ship feels near impossible to walk on. The force of the wind is incredible and the hat I was wearing is blown off, never to be seen again. I understand in an instant why Darmour had commanded the sails to be stowed. I dread to think how the mast would have coped with such pressure.

"Captain, make sure ye steer us into the waves," Darmour bellows.

"I'm trying, that sail is dragging us to the side though," Ulrik calls back.

I see where he means. Despite it being one of the smaller sails, it has sought the wind and is causing the back end of the ship to drag.

"With me!" Darmour rushes towards the sail and Orjan, Marik, and Doran follow. I head towards them but lose my footing as we crash into another large wave. I slide down the deck, only stopping when a hand grabs hold of the back of my shirt. I look up to see Yigress smiling at me. An icy cold wave crashes over us and my chest pounds as I am helped back to me feet.

"That was too close," Yigress says.

"What do you mean?"

"We need to hit the waves dead-on to make it through them. If we don't, the force of the ocean will capsize us."

"That's why they need to stow that last sail."

"Yes, if that sail causes us to turn sideways and another wave like that hits us, we'll end up in the locker!"

"We need to help them." But how? The sail in question is above where Ulrik stands at the helm. His focus is purely on the waters in front of us and I can see his arms are straining under the force to keep us on track. I head towards him, my balance all over the place as we continue to rock wildly. The rain lashes against me, the wind howling like an untamed beast. The steps are slippery but I use the railing help ensure I do not fall.

Ulrik is struggling. Yigress overtakes me and lends him a hand gripping hold of the wheel to try and hold us steady.

"Grab the rope and heave like Asterith's gold is waiting for you!" Darmour leads, pulling on the rope with Orjan, Marik, and Doran behind him. It is in vain. The force of the wind is too powerful and the sail remains outstretched.

"We're dragging!" Ulrik cries. He stands firm despite the storm throwing everything it has at him.

"Wave incoming!" Navi screams, still tethered to the crow's nest at the top of the mast, and it is a good job she is. I see the wave and my heart sinks to the pit of my stomach. We are not pointed towards it, we are being forced sideways.

Darmour lets go of the rope and rushed towards the smaller mast. Unsheathing his sword, he hits it against the rope hard enough that his blade becomes stuck in the wood. The rope is cut, and Orjan, Marik, and Doran fall into a heap, the sail flipping up and beginning to flap in the wind, no longer bound by the force that had captured it.

"Brace yourselves! This wave is going to be our biggest test yet!" Darmour commands.

My eyes are drawn to the wave that approaches us, its height reaching the skies.

Ulrik continues to fight with the wheel alongside Yigress, and the ship begins to slowly turn towards the wave as it fast approaches. I step towards the mast and take hold of some rope which is wrapped around it, rolling my wrist until it is bound tight.

"May Asterith know that I am proud to have sailed with ye all." Darmour grins wildly as if he is savouring the storm. "May the gods know that in the face of danger, we did not cower, we laughed!" He begins laughing manically, almost forcefully. He is trying to keep the spirits of our crew up, and I admire him for it.

Everyone roars in agreement as the ship crashes into the foot of the wave. We are still slightly at an angle, but Ulrik is able to get the front of the ship to hit the wave.

The force causes my head to crack forward violently. My shoulder jolts as the rope around my wrist prevents me from being hurled overboard. It digs into my skin, but it is a pain I can bear.

"Stand firm!" Ulrik roars as we begin to climb the wave, the ship leaning backwards at an unnatural angle.

My stomach sinks to its pits and every scenario, every step that has led to this moment flashes through my mind. I try to heed the advice I gave Esara and turn my fear into courage. I open my eyes and stare down the wave in front of us. We will make it through, we will survive this. For the first time I believe, for the first time I will not let my own fear consume or control me.

My attention snaps to a stray plank of wood which has torn up from the front of the ship. It flies through the air towards us at incredible speed and catches Darmour across the chest. He loses his footing and falls backwards, rolling violently towards the tail end of the ship. Out of nowhere, Orjan leaps across and grabs hold of him, and the two of them begin to slide. Orjan reaches outward and is able to snatch up some rope that is trailing from the mast. Unable to help them, I pray that the rope holds firm as they continue to slide downwards. With a snap, they stop, and Orjan holds them stable, the rope gripped tightly in one hand and Darmour in the other. For a moment they are suspended in air before the ship begins to level as we breach the top of the wave. The ship then surges forward and as we reach the bottom, the entire boat shudders. For a moment I feel the force will cause the ship to splinter into pieces and we will be lost to the ocean, but it does not. The water crashes over us once again and Orjan and Darmour roll away from the rear of the ship in a crumpled heap.

"Ye saved me!" Darmour picks himself up as the ship levels out. He is clearly in pain, but he is alive at least.

"I nearly left you. There would be no honour in that, though."

The two exchange a firm handshake.

Darmour turns to face out over the front of the ship. "I think we are through the worst of it! Keep going though, we are not out of this storm yet."

I believe what he says. These waters are still treacherous, but if we can survive a wave like that, then nothing is going to stop us reaching Treventine.

# 31
## ULRIK

'*It is a terrifying thing the ocean. A rare thing that can show equal calmness as much as chaos on the whim of the winds. It's untameable, ferocious and unforgiving when not respected.*'
*Diary entry of Darmour - 250 KR*


The gods appear to have taken favour with us over the last month, and we now find ourselves nearing the shores of Treventine. The waters have been kind to us, and we are yet to be greeted with any more storms since Yugo's Tears.

Perhaps sailing in an unnamed ship is not such bad luck, after all.

The crew has bonded together and their range of skills have made managing this ship that much easier. Darmour has played a key role in this. The crew trust him and follow his leadership and he has stayed true to his word to be my first mate.

Even Orjan has proven his worth on our journey, his reliance on ale becoming less apparent the longer we have been aboard. I can see he is helping hoist the sails. I would say that he very quickly learned what it takes to be a member of a crew, despite having no recollection of how he got to Voraz.

As I make my way across the deck, Yigress and Marik cast me polite nods. I skip up the steps to the quarterdeck where Darmour stands at the wheel, eyes fixed on the open waters ahead of us. His grey beard has thickened through our journey, his appearance having grown unkempt over the weeks. The same could be said for the rest of us; my own stubble has also begun to thicken.

"Captain." Darmour acknowledges me as I reach him, but his eyes remain fixed on the calm waters.

"Good morning, Darmour, have you been on all night?"

His eyes are purpled underneath, indicating his tiredness.

"I'll be fine, captain. Doran has been at the helm most the night. I've only been on a few hours."

I do not know whether his words are true, but his face is gaunt and pale from the lack of sleep. "You need to rest ,Darmour."

"Aye, captain, we are but a short distance from the shores of Treventine now. I will rest when we land."

I know from past experience not to waste my breath. "Very well. Have you seen my sister and Zerina?"

Darmour casts me a disapproving look. "I believe they're below deck with the knight."

Esara and Zerina have become well acquainted with Orjan. They must see something in him that I do not, but I trust Zerina. If she is okay with him, then so am I, especially after his heroic through Yugo's Tears. "Why do you still struggle with Orjan? Does he not do just as much as any other man or woman on this ship?" I ask Darmour. "And, he saved your life."

Darmour makes a face. "He is a drunkard and a gambling addict. We cannot trust him. It is only a matter of time before he will neglect his duties to fill his belly with ale or rum. When that happens, he will put us all at risk. Zerina, Esara, everyone."

"Are we not pirates, Darmour?"

He responds with a quizzical look, his gaze finally shifting from the horizon.

"Do we not all drink ale and gamble? I am sure you and your crew have seen or done far worse in your time." I am surprised at how I have challenged him, my own words backed with a stern approach.

"I trust my crew with my life. I don't trust him. Relying on him will bring nothing but disappointment, this I promise you. It is decision you will come to regret, captain. Don't let them get too attached."

"Leave me to worry about my sister and Zerina, Darmour," I reply heatedly.

"Captain." Darmour's reply stops the conversation and I can tell he no longer wishes to discuss the matter. I cannot imagine what more Orjan must do to gain Darmour's respect.

I head below deck to see what the three of them are up to. It smells of damp down here, despite everyone's best efforts to improve the living conditions. Hammocks line the sides, so at least no one is sleeping on the cold, wet floor. The captain's quarters are by no means perfect, but compared to this place, they are a luxury.

The ship groans loudly, and the sound of the waves breaking against her are louder than I remember from when I served in the King's Navy.

*No wonder Darmour looks so tired.*

Noise coming from the bottom of the room draws my attention. I follow the dull echo of laughter into the holding cells even farther below deck, a place where only mutineers or prisoners are kept.

Small torches light the area, revealing a barrel that has been turned into a makeshift table. Orjan sits illuminated next to it, Zerina and Esara opposite him. Their faces are lit up with beaming smiles.

"No way, I definitely had the right card!" Esara exclaims, giggling uncontrollably. "Zerina, you saw, I definitely picked the right card!" She brings her hand up to her head and begins to rub it, as if nursing an injury. "I want to try again."

"Very well, little miss." Orjan smiles and flashes his cards to reveal a King, a Queen, and a Jack. "Remember, you need to find the Queen. Keep your eyes on this card." He points to the overturned Queen before rotating the cards quickly. He waves his hands over the top of the cards whilst wiggling his fingers, as if casting a spell.

Esara beams with delight, her eyes filled with wonder. So much so that I do not wish to disturb them. I stand in the darkness, my arms folded tightly as I observe them. Orjan continues to bamboozle Esara, moving the cards at an increasingly fast pace until he eventually stops, spreading his arms out wide as if presenting a prize.

Esara raises her hand to her chin as she surveys the cards, then lifts her eyes to Orjan, smiling. "That one, the Queen is definitely there." She points to the card farthest away.

Orjan raises a sceptical eyebrow before slowly moving his hand over the card that Esara has chosen. "Now, you are sure you followed the right card?"

Esara nods like an over eager parrot and Orjan flips the card over.

"Not again!" Esara exclaims.

"Care to try, madam?" Orjan's attention turns to Zerina. "It's a fifty-fifty chance. Easy, is it not?"

Zerina's body language seems coy, but after a moment of surveying the cards, she points to the one in the centre. "This one, I followed it from the start."

Orjan flips it to reveal the King.

Zerina and Esara both clap, and Orjan feigns a bow. I am just about to alert them to my presence when Esara begins to speak once more.

"I think you are mistaken, Orjan." She lowers her hand over the top of the Jack, covering its picture. She concentrates for a moment, then smiles at Orjan and removes her hand, her grin even wider than it before.

"What in the gods? How did you – that is the Queen?" A Queen sits where the Jack was only moments before.

"It's my own trick," Esara teases playfully.

"Esara, you must be careful with your magic," Zerina warns.

I feel a rush of blood to my head.

"How long?" I bellow, startling the trio. "Tell me, how long have you known?"

Esara promptly recovers from her surprise. "A couple of years," she says defiantly.

"I was not talking to you!" I fix my eyes on Zerina, who averts her gaze.

"Ulrik, don't talk to her like that. I am not doing any harm with this magic!"

I ignore her. "How long have you known, Zerina?" Has she been helping Esara with her magic all this time? I have seen the affliction it causes, and I will not have my sister being exposed to it.

Orjan raises his hands. "Maybe calm down a little, captain, your sister means no harm."

"Do not tell me how to parent my sister, knight!" I scold him, my hands clenched so tightly I feel my knuckles crack.

"I do not need you to be a parent, Ulrik, I need you to be my brother!" Esara screams, tears forming in her eyes. It is not enough to stay my anger.

"Do you want to end up a haggard witch, crippled with affliction, Esara? This is how magic use starts. Little tricks like this, and before you know it, you end up in agony like Zerina, or even worse, her sister!"

Zerina's head bolts up and her eyes meet my own. Sadness quickly replaces her anger, and she barges past me, hitting me in the shoulder as she retreats.

"Zerina, wait, I didn't mean to!" I call after her, but my words go unacknowledged.

"Look what you've done! How dare you speak to her that way! How dare you, Ulrik!" Esara scowls at me, her face reddening with rage. "You are nothing but a dirty boo slugger!" she screams as she too storms past me. But for my sister, merely barging past me is not enough, and she pushes me with as much force as she can muster, causing me to stumble backwards into the hull of the ship.

All that is left is Orjan and me, with nothing but an awkward silence filling the air void between us. Orjan coughs and knocks his knuckles lightly on the barrel, the dull tap irking me further. I stand, unsure what to do. Have I overreacted? All I want is for my sister to be safe, and her magic puts her at risk.

"You speak of this to no one," I demand as I begin to

follow Esara and Zerina back to main deck. The last thing I want now is a spectacle in front of the rest of the crew.

What I do not understand is why the remedy did not work.

A ringing sound coming from the main deck is loud enough to snap my attention back.

"Do you hear that?" Orjan asks. I nod before setting off at pace, my adrenaline spiking. There's only one reason the bell would be rung.

Someone is coming.

# 32

## ZERINA

My anger engulfs me with as much fury as the flames that I can draw upon through my magic. I can understand Ulrik's concern about Esara's use of magic, because I share it. But I am unsure if I can forgive him for the way he addressed me. Is that how he sees me? As someone worth less than himself? Such pompousness is not something I am familiar with in Ulrik, nor is the spite in his tongue.

The steps to the surface move below me as if I glide over the top of them, the sea air hitting my face as soon as I rise from below deck.

"Zerina, Zerina," Esara calls after me, but for now I wish to be left alone. At least until I have calmed myself. "Zerina, why do you ignore me?"

Esara's calls break my heart further. I do not wish to upset her, or for her to feel that she has done anything wrong. I do not want her to see me upset but more importantly, I do not want my magic to consume me whilst I am in this state of anger. With us being on a boat, flames would be the worst thing for the situation.

Heading for the captain's quarters, I move as fast as my legs can take me, stifling my sobs. I wish to keep my mood free from the rest of the crew.

"Miss, are you okay?" I bump into Darmour, who places his hands on each of my arms to stop me in my tracks.

"I'm fine." It is impossible to hide my lies.

"Zerina!" Esara rises to the top, her own eyes streaming with tears.

"What in the blazes is going on?" Darmour demands, taking in the situation with concern and bewilderment. "What has that damn knight done to you both!" He removes his hands from me and is about to storm down below deck when a bell starts to ring loudly from above us in the crow's nest.

I had not noticed the thick fog that engulfed our surroundings. It is as if we are sitting in the clouds with nothing but the world below us.

"What does that mean?" I ask.

"It means there is a ship." It is Esara who answers my question. "Yigress told me."

"Even with the fog we should have seen it coming," Darmour says. "It's not a good sign if ships are able to sneak up on you."

No sooner has Darmour finished his words, the dark ship draws up close beside us, the wood of which is in a far better condition than our own. I can see many men and women aboard, all of which have their weapons bared and pointed in our direction.

"Stay your weapons!" a voice blows. It takes me a few moments to see the person who calls us. I presume he is either the captain of the ship or the first mate, though I am still unfamiliar with how these commands work, even after my time aboard this ship.

"We believe you intend to find something that should not be found." The man speaking is powerfully built, with long blond hair tied back. He wears a black and yellow military overcoat with a black tricorn hat. His skin is aged and cracked, like a cliffside weathered by the sea. He is not the tallest of men, but he is quite clearly of high command for this ship.

My heart beats faster, my anger towards Ulrik the least of my concerns. Esara tucks herself into my side and I comfort her. In this moment, the confident young spitfire is reduced to a scared child, and she buries her head into my side.

Ulrik rises from below and joins us on the main deck, his eyes surveying the ship. He furrows his brow as if he realises something.

"Captain!" Ulrik salutes the man on the other ship, a nervousness overcoming him that I have never seen. Much like his sister, the confidence he usually carries vanishes in an instant.

"Ulrik, is that you?" The captain draws closer to the edge of his boat to take a better look, his face looking even more wrinkled as he strains his eyes. His look soon turns to disappointment and then contorts with anger. "Stupid boy!" he balls across. "You were pardoned! Why on earth have you turned to piracy? Was this always your plan? To say I thought better of you is putting it mildly. It is a shame you have chosen to throw your life away so foolishly."

"Is it foolish to do what I must to stop my sister being butchered in front of an audience baying for her blood?" Ulrik calls across the water. "Where she saw our mother being slaughtered like a dog?" His face reddens, and a thickened vein protrudes from the side of his head. "From where

I stand, I am a man who will do whatever it takes to protect those that I hold dearest."

Ulrik's words resonate with me, that fire in his heart ignited by the love he has for his sister. He has thrown his life away in order to protect her. It is perhaps his most admirable quality.

"Witches!'

"Throw them overboard!"

"Let the sea have them!"

The jeers that come from the opposing crew cause my blood to run cold, an icy chill trailing down the veins in my arms. They cheered like this when they executed the others, when they murdered my sisters. Our only crime was having magic in our blood, something we have no control over.

The rush of anger builds inside me. "How dare you!" I call out. "All of you! Who are you to decide our fates? You are not gods, you are mere men!" I will not let any harm come to Esara or to the other people aboard our ship.

I look down at my hands and focus my mind, feeling my magic begin to light up my palms. "I would like to see you try and take me," I snarl, a new air of confidence in my words. "I will not be dictated to by any man. I am through with wandering the world as if I am some damsel in distress, I am far from that. I have been blessed with a gift from the gods, and I will use that gift to avenge my sisters, to avenge Ulrik and Esara's mother. More importantly, I will not let you take her, and I will not allow anyone to threaten her."

"See, she's a witch!" The screams of anger and hatred towards me intensify, and it only takes me a moment to figure out why.

There is a glow about me, one which causes my own crew to back away. Not everyone is familiar with magic like

Ulrik and Esara. My fingers tingle and my hands burst with flames as my anger begins to engulf me. I let the magic in, let it course through my blood. I am powerful and in control. The fear that consumed me is replaced with confidence. It is I who holds the cards in this situation. These men and women do not scare me, they should fear me.

"You will not take her!" my voice echoes between the two ships as the situation becomes increasingly charged, my heart beating faster.

"Zerina," Ulrik attempts to reach through to me, holding out his hand. "Let's not escalate the situation."

It is not me who is escalating the situation, it is these griffs. It is these monsters who have chosen to focus on the two witches, rather than the stolen ship and the crew that man it.

"Escalate!" I bring my flaming hand up in front of my face and carefully examine the flames that kiss my skin. "These beasts threaten to take your sister, yet I am the one escalating the situation?" My anger continues to surge like the growing waves around us.

"Get them!" Ulrik's former captain commands his crew, and in an instant they begin to rush at us, swinging from their ship onto the decks of our own.

"At arms!" Darmour rallies our own as he unsheathes his blade and slices the midriff of one of the invaders. The sailor's grip loosens from his rope, and he lands naturally on the deck of the ship, his blood pooling where he lies.

The battle cries of our crew and the metallic sound of their swords fill the air, followed by the sound of blade against blade as they begin battle with our attackers.

"Esara, get behind me, I will not let them harm you!" I yell. She moves behind me, and Ulrik moves to stand by my side.

A man lunges at me whilst grunting loudly, his face contorted with hatred. Before his blade has a chance to land, Ulrik parries it away before striking the man across the face with his free hand. The man swings at me again, and Ulrik again sways its course, knocking it away with his sword.

"Go below deck!" Ulrik commands me. There is a panic in his eyes, which unnerves me. "I do not want Esara to see this, she is only a child."

"I can help!" Esara steps out from behind me and reveals her dagger, which she clutches tightly. "I can fight."

Seeing Esara so willing to step into the fight calms my anger and helps me focus. I cannot allow her to lose her childhood seeing blood spilled. "Esara, go below deck as your brother asks."

"But what about you?" Esara asks, her body shaking.

The sailor attempts to end me once more, and this time, I lunge forward myself. I grip the man's sweat-filled face with both my hands and focus my magic. Turning towards Esara, I give her as stern a look as I can muster. "Go. I will not allow any person past this point."

The man's skin begins to crackle and sizzle under my palms. He squeals like the pig that he is.

I do not want Esara to see this, to see my rage. "I said go, Esara! Do as your brother asks."

With this, Esara disappears down the stairs and to safety, but she will only remain safe if we are able to fight off these men and women who continue to flood our boat.

I switch my attention back to the man in my grasp, the heat within my hands intensifying as I grit my teeth. He grabs my wrists and attempts to prise my hands from him, his skin instantly smoking as soon as it meets mine. He begins convulsing in agony.

I am oblivious to the carnage around me as I stare deep into the man's dark hazel eyes. I see the fear, the pain, the anguish. The wish for it all to end. I savour every last second of it. For too long have I lived in fear, for too long have those with magic been treated horrendously. It ends now. I will run no longer.

The man's eyes suddenly go blank. Ulrik stands to the side of him, his blade plunged deep into the man's torso. Blood begins to spill from his mouth, and his body becomes limp. He slumps to the floor with a thud.

# 33

## ULRIK

'*Mermaids are a creature not often seen but feared non the less. They are known to drag sailors to the depth of the ocean where they will use them to reproduce. Before devouring their flesh.*'
*Entry from magic and monsters volume IV - 199 KR*

I cannot bear to see the man's suffering any longer. The hatred in Zerina's eyes scares me. I grasp the hilt of my blade toughly as the man's lifeless body falls to the ground in front of Zerina. He attempted to end her life, but he did not deserve the pain and torment he endured in his final moments. Zerina draws her breaths quickly, her eyes wide at what she has done. I see no remorse in her actions. If anything, she seems as though she is far from finished with her magic.

"Why did you show him mercy? It is far from what he deserves." Her words are cold. This is not the Zerina I have come to know.

Before I have a chance to speak, another sailor swings

his sword, this time at me. I parry the attack with ease. He must be only in his late teens, and as we exchange a flurry of blows, I push him backwards, reluctant to end his young life. I once served on the very ship that now attacks us, around the same age as my assailant.

The young man is suddenly catapulted backwards as a ball of flames crashes into his chest. I am close enough to hear his bones crack. He is dead before he hits the floor, the blast of energy forcing its way through his chest.

"Why do you hesitate?" Zerina scolds me. "These men do nothing but threaten us, yet you hesitate to end them." With this, Zerina forces her hands together to form another ball of fire, aiming this at a woman who charges at Darmour with a pike. The woman folds in half as Zerina's magic engulfs her. Her skin chars instantly, her life ended in a moment.

I must stop this fight, I must get to the captain before both our ships end up at the bottom of the ocean. Zerina stands her ground, firing blasts of fire at anyone who gets too close to her, or anyone who makes an attempt to follow Esara.

A sword nearly takes my head clean off as yet another sailor takes a wild swing at me. I duck it before ramming the hilt of my sword into his nose as hard as I can. The over-weight man's nose explodes and his warm blood splatters against my face. I throw another punch with my free hand, and the man falls, losing consciousness.

Ahead of me, Orjan takes on three attackers by himself, fending them off with his morning star, a far cry from the drunken mess that came aboard this ship. He fights in a brutal manner, not waiting for the two men and woman to attack him, swinging his morning star with ferocious force.

As one blocks, he moves to the next with an equally powerful swing before slamming his elbow into a third person. He appears to be fighting in the same manner as myself, opting to not take the lives of those that he fights against, despite the great disadvantage this places us in. After all, how is it a fair fight when one fights to kill and the other does not?

Orjan lets out an almighty roar as he runs at one man, forcing his shoulder into his midriff before lifting him from his feet and hurling him over the side of the boat.

"ULRIK!" Captain Athorn bellows, his sword outstretched and pointing towards me. "You will pay for your treason!"

"Captain, I will do what I must to protect my sister. I do not want to quarrel with you. End this and we will be on our way," I call to him through the chaos. Maybe there is a way through to him, a way to make this stop without any further bloodshed.

"You have stolen a ship and harbour two witches. You are nothing more than a dirty, flea-infested pirate. You will swing with your sister!" Athorn charges towards me and I have no option but to engage in combat with him.

He begins to rain down blows on me, and each time I parry away his sword, he is at me with another swing. The sensation of steel against steel vibrates in my hand. Maintaining a defensive stance, I refuse to fight back beyond protecting myself. The captain is skilled with a sword, and I can feel a dull ache at the top of my arms as I begin to grow fatigued, but I know I cannot give in.

Around us, the ringing out of metal against metal mingles with screams as my crew continues to fight against my former captain and his men. Men and women being scorched by Zerina's magic wail in agony as she continues to show no mercy. I need to find a way to stop her before she slaughters everyone.

"Captain, she will end you all. I need you to stop your men," I try in vain to make this man see reason.

"Fall back!" a voice calls from behind the captain, someone who can clearly see this fight will not end well for them.

"Stay that order!" Athorn roars, furious at his next-in-command calling for his crew to retreat. He takes his fury out on me as he tries to impale me with his blade, managing to nick my shirt. Instantly I feel a burning sensation. He has sliced through to my skin, although not too deep as to need immediate attention. I raise my hand up to my side to check, and see it dripping with my blood.

The captain takes confidence in this and attacks me once more. Losing my footing, I drop backwards as the captain brings his sword down on me. I manage to roll out of the way but only just, stopping as I roll into a barrel. Wide-eyed, the captain grins at me as he stands over me and brings his sword above his head. It is the last action he takes before his life ends.

Blood begins to pool in his mouth. He gives the look of shock, dropping his sword before collapsing to his knees.

My own eyes widen as I see a panicked Esara standing behind him, dagger clenched in hand. The colour drains from her face. She loses grip of her weapon and it drops to the floor, her gaze fixed on the man she has slain. Although I am grateful to still be alive, it pains me to know that Esara has taken a life, what the guilt will do to her. I wish it was anyone but her who saved me.

The captain attempts to speak but all he can muster is a gurgling noise, spitting blood over me as he draws his last breath. Falling forward, he lands beside me, dead.

I drag myself back to my feet and stagger towards Esara, who is frozen in place, her eyes fixed firmly on the body of Captain Athorn. I bring her into my arms and hug her tightly, not only to give her my thanks and comfort her, but to prevent her from seeing the death around us.

Our attackers have begun to flee to their ship. Darmour, Yigress, Luke, and Navi cheer, waving their weapons in the air. Marik hauls a woman to the side of the ship and casts her overboard, and Orjan stands bent as he catches his breath, panting like a dog.

Charred bodies map the main deck, their skin still smouldering from the intense magic that Zerina has cast.

Screams start ringing out to my left and my attention is brought to the attacking ship. Light flashes. I have no idea how, but I know in an instant that Zerina has somehow managed to get aboard their ship, and by the sound of it, she is not finished with them yet.

"Zerina, fall back!" I call.

On the far side, she moves between the men, firing blasts of fire one after the other at any man or woman that so much as looks in her direction. With ruthless fury, she slays anyone close enough for her magic to reach.

Raising one of her hands, she fires a blast of magic at the sails, which burst into flame.

"She's going to sink their ship!" Darmour beams. "Serves 'em right for crossing blades with us."

"Foreign wood, burns well," Yigress states, folding her arms. Marik and Luko join her side, jaws agape at the spectacle.

Screams and shouts escape our enemies' mouths as Zerina continues with her destruction. Harrowing wails echo across, slowly being drowned out by the cracking and spitting of the flames that now engulf the ship. It does not take long before the main deck of the ship is aflame. What remains of the crew scramble to release a small boat on the far side to escape.

Zerina steps up onto the side of the ship, rope gripped tightly in her hand. She casts a merciless look behind her before swinging forward. Flailing through the air, she lands back on our ship, rolling across the deck. Wild cheers erupt from the other members of our crew.

Only Orjan and I are silent, taking in everything we have seen. Horrified by the destruction I have just witnessed, I do not know how to manage the situation. The flames are ripping through my former ship and crewmates, the smoke of which stings my eyes as the wind blows it in our direction.

"What about the ones that are getting away?" Navi peers over the side at the escaping sailors.

"Let them go. Let them tell their tales of what we can do. We will be the most feared pirates in the entire ocean." Darmour grins wildly as he helps Zerina to her feet before hugging her tightly with appreciation. "Blasts, no one will cross us again when they hear of this day. After all, who needs the gods on your side when you have Zerina!"

"Aye!" the rest of the crew cheers loudly, pumping their fists in the air.

"Search the dead, strip their weapons, and toss them overboard," Darmour commands without a moment's hesitation. "Then swab the decks. This blood isn't going to clean itself."

"Captain, we have lost Doran." Yigress stands over the body of our fallen crew member.

"We will make sure he has a seaman's burial," I say. I turn and stare at the burning ship. The wreckage crackles loudly as the flames quickly devour it. The heat kisses my face, snapping me out of my stupor as I realise we must make haste unless we wish for the flames to travel onto our own vessel.

"We need to move!" I yell, running towards the wheel.

"Aye, captain," Navi calls as she begins to climb the mast to take up her position in the crow's nest. It is almost ghost-like, the ease with which she ascends to the top.

Our ship begins to move, creating a safe space between us and the flaming inferno we have left in our wake. I have been involved in many battles, but none have been as destructive as this. A loud snap draws my attention to the burning vessel, which is followed by the cheers and jeers of our crew. The ship begins to sink into the uncharted depths below us. Strangely, the flames appear to burn for longer than they should under the water, the magic that caused them apparent.

We have little option other than to stay our course. We must continue in our search for the fountain of youth. I can only pray that we do not face the full force of the King's Fleet for what we have done on this day.

# 34
## ZERINA

I am surprised by how quickly my anger took control of me, but I feel no remorse for my actions. They all deserved to die. They would have slaughtered us like cattle had I not intervened. I am done with being targeted for the magic that flows through my veins.

Watching their ship sink satisfies me to no end. The flames flicker under the water until the darkness extinguishes what remains. My hands already feel like they are embedded in ice, my fingers arching as a deep cramp forces them to creep inwards towards my palms. As much as the anticipation of what is to come fills me with dread, I would take the same action without a moment's hesitation if I needed to. I will do whatever I must to protect those that I care about the most.

It is a lesson I wish I had learned sooner. Had I been able to wield my magic in this manner when my sisters and I were captured, maybe they would be alive on this day. They would not have had to endure the harrowing final moments that they faced.

Forcing my hands shut, I dig my nails into my palms,

which helps soothe the pain that is beginning to take over my arms. Blood drips from my clenched fists, splashing onto the deck of the ship, camouflaged by the blood-soaked floor.

The throbbing sensation creeps up my forearms, causing them to feel as if they are forged in metal, the weight of which I am unable to carry. Not wishing for anyone to see me in this state, I make for the captain's quarters. As I attempt to move, my legs have a different idea, and they buckle, causing me to fall forward.

"Whoa there." Ulrik moves quickly to wrap his arms around me, preventing me from falling. I am grateful for his kindness. "Are you okay, Zerina?" His concern for me seems real.

"The magic, it has drawn a lot of energy from me," I explain, my voice crackling as if my lungs are filled with smoke. Orjan's eyes widen with shock at the noise.

"Magic comes with a price, Zerina. I fear for what you will pay." Ulrik scoops me off my feet and begins to carry me to the captain's quarters. "You need to rest."

Darmour steps into our path. "That was quite the show of power there, thank you. They fear you, and by the gods, they should." He removes his cap and touches it to his chest. "You were a force to behold. Myself and this crew owe our lives to you. Thank you, missy. Rest for as long as you need."

It is more than rest that I need. I know what is about to come, as do Ulrik and Esara. By morning, everyone else will, too. Ulrik pushes open the door with his boot and delicately carries me to the bed where he lays me down as gently as he can. I grimace, and a groan of pain escapes my lips. My back feels like needles have pierced my skin.

"Did I hurt you?" Ulrik's panicked expression is endearing.

"Yes," I rasp, "but it's not your fault." I attempt to smile but I have no idea what expression I muster as Ulrik continues to look at me with concern, his darkened eyes searching over me. I cannot help but feel that if he could, he would switch places with me in an instant.

"Is there anything I can do to help? To lessen the pain?" He takes my hand, but the pain is unbearable, and I cry out. My skin burns at the touch as if they are fixed in hot coals. Ulrik recoils his hand sharply, examining my form as the shivers begin to set in. The involuntary motion causes me to tremble and shake as if I have been submerged in the coldest of water, each breath causing my lungs to ache more and more.

"N-no," I stutter as I struggle to form my words. I dread to think where my affliction will take me this time. Tears form in my eyes, which feel like red hot pokers. I squeeze my eyes tightly but even that barely stops the pain that rushes over me.

"I'll fetch you some water from below deck, maybe that will help. You look like you have a fever." Ulrik exits, leaving the door ajar.

Through the gap, eyes stare into the room with looks of confusion, fear, and concern. I turn away, unable to muster a smile, and the crew quickly avert their gazes from me and set about cleaning up the mess on the main deck.

What I would give for my sisters to be here now. Bri would know what to do. After all, she nursed Lyrissa through her addiction. Now I understand why Bri always tried her hardest for us to live a life without the use of magic. As far as I know, Lyrissa could not wield the same force of magic that I can, yet it still destroyed her.

My skin fluctuates from burning hot to ice-cold, and I scream as my body shivers. I cannot stand the touch of anything against my skin. The sea is not wild, yet the room moves for me as if we are sailing in a storm. Nauseating dizziness creeps in, just as unbearable as my fluctuating heat. Rolling onto my side, I empty the contents of my stomach onto the floor, the pain too much to bear.

The door flings open, the sound of which sends a pain into my ears like a hammer.

"Here, let me help you." Ulrik rolls me onto my back, his very touch feeling like needles forcing their way into me. "I'm sorry, I just don't want you falling out of bed." He wrings a cloth with water and places it over my head. The coldness on my face is a welcome distraction from the agonising pain in my hands and the cramps in my stomach.

Then he pulls out another cloth which he places over a bottle he has fetched.

"What's that?" Or at least that is what I try to say. What leaves my mouth is nothing short of mumbled madness.

"This will hopefully help you sleep." He douses the cloth in the liquid and brings it over my mouth.

A sharp fragrance of spirit burns into my nostrils and throat. The vapour tastes vile, and for a moment, the room feels as though it is shaking, not rocking.

"Don't worry, I am not going anywhere," Ulrik murmurs.

His words become muffled as the room around us darkens.

# 35

## ULRIK

'*The first know tale of Gregor Yerald dates back hundreds of years. It is a story of how he freed a village from the first returned demons. It was here where he left gifts, imbued with magic to prevent the darkness from ever returning.*'

*Tales Of Levanthria - 222 KR*

I have been sitting by Zerina's side for a day and a half now, her symptoms finally appearing to subside. Darmour has seen to it that the main deck is clean and the bodies of the fallen cast overboard. He has also stayed our course as we continue our voyage to the fountain of youth.

Zerina has spent her time drifting in and out of consciousness. At first, I used the solvent to keep her unconscious, but as her symptoms lessen, I have used it less and less. Although knocked out, her body continues to fight the side effects of her magic use, contorting and convulsing unnaturally. Her cold shivers are sometimes replaced by hot sweats.

I would forgive the crew for thinking that we had a banshee in our ranks, given the wails and screams that have come from this room while Zerina recovers. At this stage, I am unsure if the words of comfort I offered her were heard. For now I am simply grateful that she is still here.

Zerina begins to stir, letting out an exhausted groan as her eyes flutter awake.

"Afternoon," I say. "You gave us quite the scare there."

Zerina attempts to sit up, but her arms tremble as though they will give way. I lean forward to assist and help her to get comfortable.

Zerina parts her lips to speak but her mouth is bone dry. Her eyes navigate the room in a state of confusion. I reach for the jug of water and pour some into a tankard, bringing it to her lips. Zerina's hands encase my own as she gulps down the liquid. It is the first time she has not winced at my touch since her affliction started. Her hands tremble as the water pours down her chin. When she finishes it, I fill it again and pass it back to her. This time, she is able to lift the tankard by herself as she empties its contents once more.

"How are you feeling?"

Zerina smacks her lips together. "Like I have fallen down Pendaran Hill and hit every stone, boulder, and tree on the way down." Her voice crackles as if air still struggles to find its way in, a wheeze escaping as she talks. "My chest feels tight too."

"It has been torture simply watching you. I cannot begin to imagine what it must have been like for you."

"I will be okay. And I would do the exact same again if I needed to. Your sister means too much to me, I couldn't bear to let them get their hands on her."

"Thank you." As much as I battle with the demons of seeing all those crew members perish in their pursuit of

Esara and Zerina, I could not bear to lose either of them. All my attempts at diplomacy fell on deaf, ignorant ears. "If not for you, we would not have been able to fend them off. Their numbers far outranked our own."

"Where is Esara? Is she okay?" A sense of panic touches her voice.

"She is fine. She has remained below deck under the watch of Orjan." I have spent little time with her since the battle, my attention all on Zerina. "She took a life, Zerina. The very thing I hoped she would never have to do. If not for her actions, I may well not be here lending you aid." I have cast my mind to the fight, over and over whilst Zerina recovered. The captain could not be talked down, despite my best efforts. "Diplomacy almost got me killed, almost got us all killed."

"You are a good man, Ulrik. The fact that you offered diplomacy and they cast it aside is a reflection on them and not on you." Zerina places a soft hand onto one of my own. "Do not ever lose that. You chose not to take a life. I, on the other hand, chose fear. I let it take hold of me. True, I wanted to protect Esara, but I was angry. I wanted them to pay."

Zerina's eyes fill with tears, and she searches the quarters above us as she attempts to stop herself from crying. "All my life I have lived in exile with my sisters because of the magic that runs through my veins. Something I have no control over it. My magic only ever manifested because of what the crown did to me and my sisters. If not for them, it may never have awakened. What I cannot have is the likes of your sister being enlisted, tortured, or killed. Having their innocence stripped away. I just thought of her, and what the crown has done, and I just wanted to make them pay."

"You certainly did that." The fact that some of the crew escaped on a longboat tells me that stories of Zerina's actions will already be spreading along the shoreline and within the castle walls. It is only a matter of time before we face the full might of the King's Navy for what we have done.

"Do you not agree with what I did? I mean what I say, Ulrik. I would do it again if I had to protect those closest to me."

"I think we need to find a balance, only taking lives when absolutely necessary."

"Well maybe next time people will listen when you offer diplomacy rather than ignoring your requests."

Maybe Zerina is on to something here. If stories reach the shores about what happened with the merchant navy ship, maybe next time they will be more inclined to listen to my words and less likely to seek combat. After all, we must be the only ship on the seas that has a witch as powerful as Zerina within our ranks.

"Sail with fear." I speak my thoughts out loud.

Zerina looks puzzled by my words.

"You mentioned fear governing your thoughts, your anger. Well, when word spreads of your power, any captain would be mad to cross paths with us. If we use fear to our advantage, then we may not need to fight other ships while we make sail. We avoid conflict, which means less death."

"And I need to use less magic?"

"Exactly."

There is a creak on the boards behind us and I spin quickly to find Esara eavesdropping.

"Zerina, you're awake!" She beams at the sight of her friend and speeds over, diving onto the bed. Zerina winces as she cuddles up to her, but this is quickly replaced with a

peaceful smile. It is hard to believe that someone as delicate, thoughtful, and caring as Zerina could produce such
chaos. "I missed you, I've been worried sick about you. So
have Orjan and the others."

"I will have plenty of time to catch up with everyone,
don't worry." Zerina gives Esara another squeeze, and the
two of them settle down.

"Come, sister, I am sure Zerina could do with a little
more rest." Zerina's face looks gaunt and weary. The more
rest she has now, the better we will fare when we finally
reach Treventine.

"I will fetch you some food." I pick up my tricorn hat
from the side of the bed and tip my head to Zerina. "Esara,
please come out in five minutes. It is important that Zerina
rests."

"I will, brother."

I reach the door of the captain's quarters and breathe in
the fresh sea breeze that greets me, then I hear the gulls.
Darmour stands at the helm, a brazen smile cascading
across his worn face. I approach the steps and make my
way to him. "What has you in such good spirits, Darmour?"

"We have had a good wind behind us, maybe the gods
do favour us on our quest." Darmour nods towards the
direction we sail. "Land ahoy, sir. We have reached
Treventine."

The small island lies ahead of us. Treventine, as far as
we know, is uninhabited, which means we have no idea
what awaits us once we land. "It would appear we have,
Darmour. Ready the crew. We have riches to find."

# 36
## ULRIK

We leave the ship anchored in the deeper waters, and Yigress and Marik stay behind with Esara. Zerina, Darmour, Tobias, Luka, Navi, Orjan, and I make hot to the shoreline using the longboat. I am surprised we have made it this far without sinking, such is the decrepit appearance of the boat. There is a nervousness in the air as our expedition brings us to a new destination.

"Do we know where to head when we land?" Tobias asks as he and Luko row us to the shore.

I unfurl the cloth map in my possession. The island is simply circled without other markings. There is, however, another etching of a cave, and a waterfall. "I would hazard a guess to say that it is in a deep, dark cave, just as this map was."

"This is going to be easy. We get in, find the fountain, and leave," says Navi, focussing on the land that we fast approach.

"Did Ulrik mention the map was guarded by skeleton

warriors?" Zerina smiles at Navi who in return casts a flirtatious smile back.

"Like I said, witch, it is going to be easy."

"Please do not call me that."

"Is this not what you are?" Luko's thick accent points out the obvious. "You are a magic caster?"

"I am, yes, but the term witch, I am not fond of. It is what they branded us as when they captured me and my sisters and paraded me all the way to Eltera. I find it quite derogatory."

"Sorry, ma'am, they did not mean anything by it," Darmour cuts in to stop an argument forming. Besides, they would be mad to start an argument with Zerina in such a confined space.

"Do you know anything of Treventine, Darmour?" I ask.

"As I said before, the waters surrounding it are meant to be treacherous," he replies.

We all cast looks around us, but the waters are calm and clear, and we are about fifty feet away from the beach.

"Are you sure we are in the right place, Darmour?" Zerina presses.

"Aye, I would stake my good eye on it. See those cliffs over there? That one on the right, looks like a horse drinking from the ocean, does it not?"

Sure enough, there is a rock that look like horse's head perched over and leaning into the water.

"So there is," I reply.

"Then we are at Treventine, mark my words."

Out of the corner of my eye, I see a dark shadow heading our way, too fast for me to see what it is. There is a jolt and the boat rocks slightly.

"What was that?" Navi asks, searching the waters wildly to get a better look.

Darmour eyes the sea around us. "Treacherous waters, Navi. Best keep away from the edges."

There is another knock, this time more violent, and the boat rocks, causing Navi to lose her footing and fall into the sea.

"Pull her back in, quickly!" I command. Navi splashes back to the surface, laughing and spluttering as she reaches for Tobias's decrepit hand.

He does not have a chance to pull her up as the boat is slammed again, this time with enough force to tip it on its side and send us all overboard.

Water blasts into my face and I lose my bearings as I sink into the cold ocean. Water forces its way up my nose, causing a deep sting. I kick my legs to bring me to the surface as quickly as I can, gulping for air when I do, trying not to panic but panicking all the same.

My mind races. What it is that has cast us all overboard? Orjan is the next to reach the surface alongside Navi, who appears to be grateful for the company. One by one the others begin to pop out of the water, Darmour, Zerina, Tobias. We all cough and splutter as we face one another, searching around us for whatever creature is responsible for this.

"Where's Luko?" Orjan asks.

Water sprays upwards as Luko reaches the surface for air, splashing wildly. Navi instantly starts swimming towards him, a panicked look on her face.

"I can't swim!" Luko screams.

Navi grabs hold of him to keep him afloat. "Anyone care to help?" she demands. "He is too heavy for me on my own."

Orjan swims towards them to lend them aid while Luko continues to flail around like a beached fish.

"Help me!" he calls, Navi struggling to keep hold of him. His flailing arms catch her square in the nose, causing it to bleed straight away.

"Will you keep still, you oaf!" Navi scolds him, clutching her face.

I feel something brush past my legs, and panic shoots through my body. No sooner does her blood trickle into the sea, both Navi and Luko are pulled under water.

"To the shore!" I cry. Tobias, Darmour, and Zerina begin to make way. Orjan is already swimming in Navi and Luko's direction, and I follow suit. I reach the spot and dive underwater. Navi and Luko are being pulled down by *something*.

I reach out and am able to grab her arm. I try to pull her free, and whatever has hold of her lets go. She begins to rise to the surface alongside me.

"What in god's fuck was that?" she splutters, splashing around violently.

"Head to the shore," I tell her.

Around us, the water turns crimson.

"Luko! Luko!" Navi screams.

"He's gone, Navi. We must make our way to the shore!"

There is a large spray of water between us as something fires up out of the sea. I recoil in horror as I realise it is the mangled body of Luko, his legs and an arm missing. His eyes are wide, his mouth open in shock as he slams back into the water before sinking to the depths. There is another splash, and the creature responsible makes its appearance, emerging up out of the water. Its body is that of a woman, its scaly tail of a fish. It dives, landing where Luko has hit the water, making to feast on his body.

"Mermaid!" I call out, in the hopes of getting everyone to swim faster. I pray there is only one of these creatures in our midst.

Without a moment's hesitation, we franticly swim towards the shore. Safety has never seemed so far away. If there is only one of them, Luko's body may be enough to appease it. If this mermaid is in season, it is the men of our crew that are in danger of being eaten next.

My legs burn as I swim as fast as I can, kicking hard against the water, clawing with my arms as I try to propel myself. My heart races, my thoughts darting to the danger that we find ourselves in. The shore draws closer, and with every stroke, we are a little bit safer.

There is a loud splash behind me. The creature is done with Luko.

Darmour, Navi, and I have almost drawn level with the others, age clearly on our side. Zerina swims ahead of everyone, nearly to shore.

"Keep going!" I splutter as we swim, "she's on her way!" We continue to press ahead but I cannot help but notice Tobias is slipping behind.

A shrill scream sounds as the mermaid splashes from the water again, ecstatic at her luck of having so many people in the water to feast upon. I turn briefly to see how far away she is. Unfortunately for Tobias, the mermaid is upon him. His scream of pain echoes for a brief second before he is plunged under the water.

My limbs ache like never before but I am desperate to reach the shoreline. With one last push I put everything I can into making it to safety. I have fallen behind Navi and the others. Water rises from behind me, and I know in an instant the mermaid is closing in.

Then my knees hit against the base of the sea, and I reach shallow ground. I claw and clamber until I am able to wade through the water, but it is still deep enough for the mermaid to swim though. As the water shallows, my pace picks up, and I am confident I can make it.

My foot catches a rock, sending me crashing back into the water. Panic overcomes me and I franticly try to get back to my feet, but the quicker I try, the more I lose my footing, and all I can do is land on my back facing upwards towards the sun. The ripples in the water continue to head my way, the snarling face of the mermaid facing me as she makes her way to finish me off. Her shrill scream rings out once more as she catapults herself out of the water and attempts to drag me with her, baring her blood-soaked fangs.

She shrieks again as something slams into her shoulder, embedding deeply. She slaps into the water besides me and flails around, trying desperately to slice me with her clawed hands. There is a splash from behind, and Navi is upon the mermaid. She spins her over to reveal a dagger protruding from her.

"You fucking whore!" Navi pulls the dagger out and begins ramming it into the mermaid's torso. The mermaid claws back, but Navi is unfazed by the cuts she is sustaining, and she continues to furiously stab the creature until it eventually stops flailing around. The monster's dark blue blood soaks into the sea as Navi plunges her dagger into it one last time.

We have lost two men, but we have made it to land.

Navi reaches out a hand and helps me to my feet before the two of us head to the safety of the beach to join the others.

# 37

## ZERINA

'*Woman and magic is rare combination. The history books tell us that when a woman can wield magic it brings nothing but death and destruction to the world. It is why those who can wield hide, so that they are not chastised for something which they have no control over.*'
*Harriet Clem, KR 218*

Treacherous waters is putting it mildly. Never again will I let us fall to such an oversight. The mermaid that attacked us is the most ferocious creature I have ever seen, and I never want to cross paths with one again. If not for Navi's intervention, I fear that Ulrik would not have made it to the beach.

I was powerless to draw on my magic when he needed it most.

The mermaid bobs around in the shallows of the water, eerily. Her body is now motionless, simply moving back and forth with the motion of the tide.

"We lost two good men today. Let's not make it in vain,"

says Darmour, patting Ulrik on the back. He gazes out at the open ocean, and we join him in his moment to think about our fallen crew members.

"As much as I would like to rest and gather my breath, I do not wish to wait for whatever creatures inhabit this place to find us." Navi sheathes her dagger and walks past us. "You said it is a cave we are looking for. I suggest we follow the shoreline before we head inland," she says.

I cast a look to Orjan who simply shrugs and the rest of us begin to follow Navi.

"I thought we had lost you then," I tell Ulrik, smiling. "Don't be getting any ideas. I do not want you falling at the final stage of our journey."

"All I want is a better life for my sister. If the riches here can provide that, I care not for my life. As long as she has hers."

I have only known him a short while but I know that his intentions are pure, even if it has led to us stealing a ship and becoming pirates.

"You care for nothing else, do you?"

"She is all I have. Everything I do is to ensure her a better life."

I admire him for the way he wants to protect Esara, but I wish he would realise she is not all he has. All he has to do is open his eyes and see the crew he has assembled, see that I care for him too.

"She is lucky to have you in her life. My eldest sister, Bri, always had my best interests at heart. It is just unfortunate that by the time I realised this she was already gone."

I glance at a ring on my finger that she gave me when I was younger, and notice that my hand looks wrinkled and worn, as if that of an older person. I gasp, the sight catching me off guard.

"Is everything okay?" Ulrik asks.

I draw my sleeve over my hand. "It's nothing, something just startled me, that's all." Is this the result of my magic use? I saw what it did to my sister. Her skin was aged as if she was years older than she was. My heart skips as I begin to panic, my arms and legs still aching and in recovery from my latest spellcasting.

I glance over my left hand and see the same aged skin, and when I roll up my sleeve, my forearm is just as wrinkled. In some parts the skin is cracked and weeping. I draw my hands up to may face whilst we walk and brush my fingers over my skin. Everything feels as it should.

Then it dawns on me: the magic I cast manifests from my hands. Is this why they are worn and breaking? Looking at my arms, I worry about what will happen in the immediate future if I continue to use magic so carelessly. I can only hope and pray to the gods that they will heal in time.

"Are you sure you're okay, Zerina?" Ulrik pulls me from my thoughts.

I try to smile but I am unsure if it is convincing. "I'm sure, let's keep going."

"Up here!" Navi points to a cove that lies ahead. When we reach her, she motions down to a small opening within the cove. "It appears we have found our cave entrance."

"So it would appear. Come on, let's go." Ulrik leads with Darmour and Navi.

Orjan leans into me. "I have seen your affliction in others, Zerina. No matter what happens in here, please resist your body's urges to cast magic. I worry what will happen if you do." His southern accent is more alluring now that he is sober.

"Thank you, Orjan, I think I would second your

thoughts. Here's to hoping that we do not find ourselves in a situation where my magic is needed."

"All I ask is that you do not seek an excuse to use it," Orjan tells me.

"You have nothing to worry about, Orjan." I try to brush his comments off, but the addiction is the hardest part of all this. The urge to use just that tiny bit in order to make the pain lessen.

"Heed caution to my words, Zerina," Orjan finishes before he sets off, following the others.

We make our way towards the cove, my feet dragging through the sand as if they are made of metal. Maybe it would have been better for me to remain on the ship with Esara. With two men down already, I suppose it is a good thing that so many of us headed for the shore.

The sea cascades in and out of the cove and I do not blame us for our hesitance to go near the water. All of us opt to keep a safe distance, just in case any more mermaids are lurking.

Navi waits eagerly for us at one side of the cave entrance, and Darmour stands opposite to her as Ulrik catches up with them. He stares into the dark void where we seek to explore. We must be mad, but with promise of treasure coaxing us in, who knows? Maybe a better lifestyle awaits.

Orjan finds a branch and constructs a makeshift torch. Darmour removes a small bottle from his jacket pocket and pours it over the torn fabric before using a flint to light it.

"You all ready?" Ulrik asks.

"Aye, captain," Navi replies

"Ready as we'll ever be," Darmour says, raising the torch above his head. "What are waitin' for? We've got treasure to find."

# 38
## ULRIK

As we make our way into the tunnel, the smell of stagnant water greets us, blended with the green moss that coats the cavern walls. Darmour stands just in front of me, his arm outstretched with the torch lighting the small area around us. Darkness hails us from every direction, the light from outside soon fading. The other three form behind me as we make our way farther into the cavern.

"What if the tide follows us inside?" Zerina's voice echoes.

"Then we will be fucked," Navi answers. "Let's hope there is an exit up ahead. It will be hard enough to find our way back in the darkness."

"Keep your concentration," I remind them, "we need to remain focused." Who knows what lies in here?

It is hard to keep my footing. The ground is slippery from the algae that coats everything. We continue our course, the sound of the ocean slowly disappearing with each passing wave, replaced by the occasional sound of water dripping.

We arrive at an intersection, with tunnels splaying out in three different directions.

"I feel a draft," Darmour says as the flames on the torch flicker to the side. "There's an opening this way, I'm sure of it."

I trust his judgement but ultimately, he carries the torch, so either way we need to follow him. We continue a short distance before he brings us to a stop.

"What is it?" I ask.

"There's steps."

I do not like the idea of traveling downwards in a cave. It is the journey back that concerns me more than anything.

I am right to be weary; I lose my footing and slip, landing on my backside before Orjan drags me back up from behind.

Taking our time with the remainder of the steps, we soon reach the bottom, much to my appreciation. We continue down the tunnel for a few moments, following Darmour's lead.

"Shit!" Navi's voice creeps from behind with hushed apprehension.

I stop in my tracks and turn to face her. "What's happened?"

"It's nothing, just a loose stone that I've stood on. Nearly snapped my foot." She makes to continue forward –

"Don't move, Navi!" Darmour calls, but his words are too late. She takes a step and the walls around us shake suddenly.

"Cover!" Darmour cries as a large section of wood swings out from the wall, threatening to pin us all. Instinctively, I drop to the floor, and Darmour drops the torch but I can see him lying on his chest too. On my other side, Zerina and Orjan hit the ground.

Navi is less fortunate. She stands, her legs trembling. I jump to my feet to aid her but there is nothing I can do. She is pinned to the wall by the heavy piece of wood.

"With me!" I yell. The four of us pull as hard as we can on the wood, forcing it away from her. Not only has her chest been crushed, but wooden spikes also protrude, leaving gaping holes in her torso. Blood pools in her mouth, her bulging eyes looking as though they are ready to pop out.

She falls forward. I catch her and bring her down gently to the floor. It was only a short time ago that she saved my life, and now she lies in my arms drawing her last breaths. As she breathes, her chest rattles violently, only taking in small amounts of air. She looks confused and shocked, unable to form words through the blood that fills her mouth. She splutters as she tries to breathe once more, then draws silent, as still as the shadows we form.

I bring my hand down to her face and close her eyes for the final time before laying her delicately on the ground.

"She was a good woman, a good pirate. May the gods help her find peace." Darmour salutes her from where he stands, planting a firm hand on my shoulder. "Come, we must leave. Be mindful in case there are any more traps. If anything, it means we are close. We can't afford to lose any more of us."

I am surprised at how easily Darmour moves on. Am I naive for growing attached to the crewmates who serve us?

"This way," Darmour directs us, and we continue our journey into the darkness. We move at a slower pace than before, not wishing to trigger any more traps. It isn't long before we reach an opening in the cavern and my mind goes back to the one where we found this map, the one where we awakened the dead. As we enter, the room is well lit from what appears to be multiple openings above. Beams of light illuminate where we stand, and in the centre of the cavern lies a stone table. I can see from a distance it is carved, but it is unclear what shapes are etched into it.

Leading the others, I make my way towards it, eager to see what lies in wait for us. As I approach, my heart beats hard against my chest.

Two faces are carved into the stone, one with Elvish features, most notably its pointed ears. A smile is etched onto her face, the stone polished, the intricacy of the carving clearly carved by a master stonemason. On the other side is the Elvish face of a man corrupted by a darkness. He is carved with scaled skin, sharp teeth protruding out of a slightly elongated face. Between the two, a chalice is etched into the stone.

"This must be it. This must be the point." I look around the rest of the cavern, unsure of what to do or what this means.

Zerina joins me in front of the stone table and brushes her hand over the top, removing dust and dirt that seems to be covering something.

"It's Elvish," she says.

What she reveals are words and symbols that I cannot decipher.

"Can you – "

"I think so," she replies, brushing the rest of the dirt off to reveal the full body of the inscription.

"The blood of magic, A sacrifice, Untold power awaits, Beware." She staggers her words, reading out loud slowly whilst deciphering them.

"Blasted elves. Why has there always got to be a sacrifice?" Darmour scowls at the translation.

"Pass me your knife, Darmour," Zerina says.

Bemused, Darmour removes a small dagger from his waistband and passes it to her.

"I think I know what to do." Zerina clasps one hand around the blade, wincing as she does so. Now the knife is decorated with the blood from her hand, and blood to starts to drip from her clenched fist. It splashes onto the stone table, and within moments the letters begin to glow. Whatever magic lies within this place, Zerina has awakened it. The room around us begins to rumble, and dirt falls from the ceiling onto us. We all need to quickly steady ourselves to prevent from falling.

"What's happening?" Orjan asks.

"The cave is going to fall in on itself!" Darmour shouts.

The room continues to rumble, and in the distance, I can hear something else. Something that is getting louder and louder, indicating it moves in our direction.

"Do you hear that?" I exclaim. "It sounds like water."

No sooner have I said the words, water cascades into the room, forming a waterfall at the far end of the cavern. Water rushes inwards at an alarming rate, pooling into what I now see as some form of moat carved into the stone floor surrounding the table. The room shines brighter than ever, the light from before reflecting on the clear water. The waterfall slows but still flows naturally into the room.

"This is it!" I yell. "This is the fountain of youth!"

# 39

## ZERINA

*'There are many types of magic often forgotten until recent times when King Athos decreed he wanted those with magic to join his ranks. Seer's are said to look into the future and manipulate the present. Those that cast glamours are able to change the appearance of an object. It is even possible to control the elements such as fire and ice. Necromancy however has always been forbidden even in the Diet age when magic was freely accepted, when those that could harness its power were seen as gods and goddesses.'*

*Jordell Torvin - 263 KR*

My hand throbs, but as much as its stings and causes me discomfort, it pales in comparison to what I have become accustomed to.

Everyone stands in awe of the clear blue water that now surrounds us. We have done it. We found the fountain of youth.

"What do we do next?" I ask. "It is not as though we can transport all this water back to Levanthria."

"Enjoy the moment, miss," Darmour replied, an immovable smile etched onto his face.

"The inscription read sacrifice. Your blood is the sacrifice the fountain requires?" Ulrik stands at the edge of the platform surrounding the table, staring into the waters that now surround us. He looks transfixed with his reflection.

"You look like you have never seen water before," I tease.

"I have never seen water with such a magical appearance."

We do not know yet what the water does to the body, but one can only imagine with a name such as the fountain of youth that it brings about some form of immortality. A chance to roll the years back. The question now is whether there is any truth to such tales.

"There is only one way to find out. Someone needs to drink the water," Darmour points out. "The stone table has a chalice etched into it. We shouldn't be drinking anything without first finding that chalice to drink from. I ain't taking no chances."

"I agree," says Orjan with a nod. He walks over to the blood-soaked table. "Look."

Water has pooled in the very centre of the table, mixing with my blood.

In front of the table, freshly ground stone sprinkles over the floor by my feet.

"The chalice!" I exclaim, "the chalice is right here!" Crouching down, I rub my hands over the stone carving of the chalice in between the two faces. It has become loose, which confirms my theory, and I am able to remove it from the table. It is heavy, but what can I expect when it is also carved from stone?

Instinctively, I fill the chalice with the water that has

pooled on the table. The liquid is not as thick as blood, but it remains as red as wine. "Bottoms up."

"No, Zerina," Ulrik calls and moves to stop me from drinking it. "We still don't know what it will do."

My arm stops dead in its tracks, Orjan's firm hand gripped tightly around my forearm. "No, Zerina, I will try it. I owe it to you for having faith in me." Before I have a chance to reply, Orjan takes the chalice from me and brings it up to his mouth. "Besides, it's been a while since I had a drink." He smiles and tilts the chalice towards me as though proposing a toast, then takes a drink.

He winces as he places the chalice back onto the stone table, my blood staining his top lip.

"Well, that tastes as far away from wine as you can imagine," Orjan jokes.

A look of bewilderment over comes him.

"What's wrong?" I ask.

Orjan bends over, holding his stomach., then he cries out in pain as he collapses onto the ground.

"Orjan!" I drop to my knees and roll him onto his back. His eyes are tightly shut, his face contorting with pain. His body tenses as though he is having a seizure.

"What's happening to him?" I speak panicked words as I desperately try to think how to soothe his pain.

"The sacrifice." Ulrik's words trickle from his mouth. As if not believing them himself.

"No, not Orjan. Not any of you!" Tears form in my eyes. "Not like this."

Orjan's eyes burst open, revealing yellow where whites once were. His pupils have changed too, almost diamond shaped from the top of his eyes to the bottom. This doesn't make any sense. What is happening to him?

"It hasn't killed him," says Darmour, "the water has cursed him."

Orjan releases another agonising scream, this time revealing a vast amount of small, pointed teeth. His skin begins to bubble and his face becomes deformed. I have never seen anything like this.

"Get away from me!" he cries, pushing me away as he rolls onto his side. His body twitches and contorts, and the cracking noises make me wince with every snap of a bone. It pains me that we are powerless to stop whatever is happening to him. His screams echo around the chamber, bouncing off the walls in an unwanted harmony. The writhing stops, the screams die out, and I see no movement.

An eerie silence falls over us as we all stand frozen in shock, unsure what to do. Then Orjan's side expands as though taking a deep breath, a strange rattling noise coming from him as he breathes. The pace of the breathing picks up and Orjan begins to stand. His back facing us, he is now a good foot taller than he was before, and his legs are bent at the knee. A grumble emits from him as he steadies his breathing.

He turns to face us.

I gasp at what I see. His rugged features have been replaced with scales that I can only describe as lizard-like. His eyes are a deep yellow, the centre of his face elongated to reveal a snout. The low grumble he emits turns more into a growl and he opens his mouth slightly, revealing those spiked teeth once more.

"Orjan," I call out, "Orjan, it's me."

His eyes look vacant from those that I have become accustomed to. He shakes his head whilst continuing to grunt and growl. As if battling thoughts, as if losing control of himself.

"Zerina, keep your distance," Ulrik warns me, his tone serious. He brings his hand to the hilt of his blade.

Orjan senses this and emits a frightening roar from deep within himself, and I clasp my hands over my ears at the sound. Orjan rushes towards me, raising a scaled hand which he aims to bring down on me. Ulrik dives into Orjan, preventing the blow. The two of them fall into a heap on the floor, then scramble back to their feet. Orjan looks ready to pounce on Ulrik. He weighs up the situation before reaching for his morning star and raising it high into the air.

"Orjan, I do not wish to fight you." Ulrik holds his hands up.

Orjan ignores this and takes a wild swing at Ulrik who manages to step to the side, dodging the blow.

"I do not think now is time for diplomacy, Ulrik!" I call across. "Orjan is cursed. He is not in control."

Orjan takes another swing at Ulrik, and this time Ulrik removes his sword and parries the blow. Orjan's strength now far outmatches Ulrik's, and he is barely able to keep his balance. Orjan overpowers Ulrik with a kick to his side, sending him sprawling across the ground. He stops just before hitting the water.

Orjan dives at him again but is intercepted by Darmour, who now crosses blades with him. The two exchange blows with one another, allowing Ulrik to rise to his feet. He and Darmour team up against an enraged Orjan.

It is not enough. Orjan is faster and stronger than them both. He backhands Darmour with his free hand before slicing his morning star down upon Ulrik. Ulrik again blocks this but the spiked ball barely misses his head. Orjan spins on the spot, striking Ulrik to the ground again. Orjan is too powerful for the two of them.

"*Do not seek an excuse to use magic,*" I speak out loud. The situation is not an excuse, it is a necessity. Focusing deeply, I let the magic take hold of me, and a surge of adrenaline courses through my body. I feel all my senses become heightened. The surge of energy is amazing. All the aches in my body cease in an instant, the pain in my hand replaced with a gentle throbbing sensation that feels soothing. My magic courses through me, emitting an eerie force that lifts the dirt from the ground around me.

I focus my thoughts to my hands, sending a surge of flames towards Orjan. I do not wish to hurt him, but I need to keep him away from the others. My magic misses Orjan, firing into the ground just behind him. It is enough to catch his attention and he spins to face me, roaring in my direction and making his way towards me.

I fire two more blasts at him, not as powerful as I can muster, but enough to subdue him. The flames bounce off him, delaying his steps, but only by seconds. He is soon upon me, and he swings his morning star. Drawing all my energy into my hand, I deflect the weapon away from me. Slamming my free hand into Orjan's chest, I make some distance between the two of us but only for a moment. He is relentless in his assault. I place my hands on his chest, my hands searing his plate armour. My hand starts to push into the metal. Orjan snaps at me as though wild and on the hunt, his warm breath greeting my face. I see each of the many jagged teeth that line his mouth and I fear the monster he has become.

"Orjan, please stop," I tell him. He grips my shoulders, his pointed nails burying deep within my skin. He pushes me backwards and I bounce over the stone table, sending the chalice hurtling through the air and into the water that surrounds us. Orjan dives through the air towards me and I force all my magic into my legs, somehow channelling the force to kick him away.

Ulrik and Darmour grab his arms, struggling wildly as they attempt to hold him steady. My body grows weak. I am still not recovered from my overuse of magic and here I am again, channelling it through my body. I feel my magic dampening, my hands slowly losing the flames that have wrapped around them. The icy pain returns, forcing my fingers to bend inwards against their will.

"Zerina, are you okay?" Ulrik calls, still struggling against Orjan's increased strength.

"I don't feel so good." My head feels faint, and I stumble backwards. It is clear I have broken my body, and now my magic runs dry.

"Zerina, your face, your hair!"

My hands tremble uncontrollably. They are withered and bony. The hands I stare at are those of an elderly lady near death, not a nineteen-year-old woman. I press my fingers to my face and feel the wrinkles that have formed there. Panic overcomes me and I lose my footing.

"Zerina!" Ulrik cries out. The room spins around me as I tumble through the dirt.

Water surrounds me. For a moment I allow myself to simply float, the weightlessness bringing a sense of relief to my broken body. Fragmented light from above washes over me, guiding me back to the surface. My legs, however, have other ideas. I find myself exhausted and unable to kick, and I remain submerged. Closing my eyes, I accept my fate.

My body jerks as I run out of air. Unable to move and suspended in the water, I fear what will happen to Ulrik, Darmour, and Orjan.

"Zerina." The voice is as clear as if someone stands in front of me. "Zerina, let go, it's time to let go." It is Lyrissa. She is calling me. Her voice soothes me like no one else can. Closing my eyes, I embrace meeting my sisters in the afterlife.

# 40
## ULRIK

"ZERINA!" My voice grows hoarse as I scream loudly, not that my words will change anything. Zerina has fallen into the water, her frail, aged body too fragile to cope with the burden of magic any longer. My attention is snapped back to Orjan who continues to struggle. If it was only my life that mattered, I would let go, but for now Darmour and I need to work together.

"Keep hold of him, Ulrik, the beast grows tired."

I know not of what Darmour speaks as I desperately try to hold on to Orjan's arm and prevent him from striking either of us.

Feet scramble against the dirt as we all fight to maintain control. Orjan is far away from the fallen knight he once was.

Darmour loses his grip and Orjan breaks his arm free, swinging his hand around to my side. His clawed hand makes contact as his fingers embed into my stomach. Using both my hands, I pull his claws away, and Darmour slices him down his armour, adding further damage, though it is clear that Darmour is holding back. Like me, he does not wish to do any permanent damage to Orjan, but I fear we will soon not have a choice.

Ignoring my injury, I reach for my sword and we both take swings at Orjan's armour, each blow causing him to step back as he attempts to shield himself. We continue this until we reach the centre stone.

When will this end? How do we stop this? We have lost so many on this voyage, and what for? A cursed knight and two injured pirates?

Water sprays to my left, causing my attention to drift. I stand in shock as Zerina emerges at the edge of the water, panting heavily, her sharp blue eyes fixed on Orjan. Her skin is no longer aged and cracked; her greying hair has returned to its usual jet-black form.

"The fountain, it – it works!" Darmour grins as he forces Orjan back with his blade.

Zerina runs in our direction and clasps her hands tightly around Orjan's head. She mutters an incantation which I assume is Elvish, over and over. Orjan is paralysed in an instant, his body becoming less tense, his arms no longer flailing.

"Step away from him," says Zerina, then continues her incantation as she leaps backwards from him. Orjan brings his hands up as if swatting flies around his face. He growls and falls, slamming into the ground.

"What did you do?" I ask.

"I cannot fully lift the curse, but I have given him his mind back."

"And where did you learn to do that?" Darmour follows up as he sheathes his sword and brings his hands up to his hips, trying to catch his breath.

Zerina simply points at the water. "The fountain has cleansed me from the damage caused by using magic."

I rush forward and hug her, squeezing her as tightly as I can. "I thought I had lost you." Zerina wraps her arms around me.

"I thought I was gone too. The fountain, it spoke to me," she says. "My sister Lyrissa calmed me, soothed me. She told me to accept my fate. To let go. I did what she asked, and I embraced the darkness, I allowed myself to slip away, thinking I was greeting my sisters in the afterlife." Zerina does not appear as though she has used any form of magic in this fight, nor does she appear to be succumbing to any symptoms.

"It was not darkness that greeted me," she continues, "it was light, knowledge. All at once, I can't explain. Magic, its uses, the different kinds, it is as if all the knowledge the elves had of magic has flooded into my mind. Everything feels so much clearer."

"What do you mean?" I ask her, finally pulling away, though I do not want to let her go.

"The fountain's ability, why it was created over a millennia ago. The elves struck a deal with the gods. They wanted a way to stop magic from destroying their bodies, from the affliction breaking them. Their pleas for help were answered by the god of water, Nen, who bestowed on them the waters that surround us. The waters will negate the effects of magic use for those that drink from it."

"So using magic causes your body to break down and age you beyond your years. Drinking from the fountain reverses that." I think I understand what Zerina is saying.

"That is correct. Not only this, those that drink from the fountain receive all the knowledge of those that have wielded it before," she explains. "There is a catch though.

Nen, not wanting the fountain to be misused, ensured that only people who have magic within their bodies could drink from it. To protect it from overuse, a sacrifice needs to be made by a willing body, someone who does not carry magic."

That explains Orjan then. He has been cursed to activate the powers which lay dormant in the water. Zerina's cleansing has come at his expense. "Can it be reversed? The effects on Orjan, can they be reversed?" I ask.

"I have used what magic is known, what the elves have been able to pass onto me. It would appear they figured out how to release someone's mind from the curse, but not the body. It is why they sealed this place. The cost was too high to use the fountain's waters."

"So ye mean Orjan is trapped in this form?" Darmour asks.

"It means that a spell strong enough to reverse the curse has not been found yet. It does not mean it cannot be done. I will break this curse. I will find a way. For now, we need to get him back to the ship."

"He was a foolish man to drink from the chalice. A brave man, but a foolish man nonetheless." Darmour walks to Orjan who lies unconscious on the ground, and gestures for us to assist him.

I lean down and pull him to his feet, casting his arm over my shoulder, his scaled face next to my own. I can only hope that Zerina is correct in her words and her magic has broken his mind free. The last thing I want now is for him to wake, and in his feral state, bite down on my face. I press my free hand to my side where blood oozes from Orjan's strike.

"Yer injured, captain." Darmour's eyes fix on me.

"I will be fine, we need to get to shore."

"Let me take a look." Zerina kneels and raises my shirt to examine my wound. She places her hand over the top and starts mumbling words that I do not know the meaning of. I wince as the pain in my side intensifies, Zerina's hand burning hot against my skin.

"My magic isn't working," she says. "There is something wrong with this wound. I've just tried sealing it with the heat of my power but it remains open. This was inflicted by a cursed hand, and I fear that your wound is bound by dark magic. We need to get back to the ship quickly so I can try and heal you." She frowns, perplexed.

I have trust in Zerina, and I agree with what she says. "Come on, we need to get back to the surface before Orjan wakes up." The throbbing in my side takes my breath away, but I have every faith that Zerina can fix it.

# 41

## ZERINA

'The island of Voraz is often seen as a place filled with deplorable pirates, people who would sell their soul if it fetched enough coin. True these types do exist, however I come to find more honour and trust amongst these people than those who govern our kingdoms.'

*Diary entry oh Ulrik Thatch - 262 KR*

Yigress and Marik have managed to steer the ship into the cove, granting us easier access to the ship, although the thought of another mermaid attack is fresh on our minds. Once we winch Orjan back on board, we stand around him on the main deck.

"Orjan!" Esara is beside herself. "He has the scales of a dragon!"

She is right. His skin has been replaced by the scales used to create dragons, the mythical creatures that once roamed these lands. These have been reduced to nothing more than tales of old, but now that I have drunk from the fountain, I understand these tales to be true.

"We will find a way to fix this, Esara, I promise you this. I will not rest until this curse is broken. The fountain works. I can use magic with no effect on myself. I will use this to our advantage, to cure him."

"At what cost though, Zerina?" Esara cries. "Orjan may never be the same again."

"We will make it our very purpose to exist, sister. We will find a way to undo the magic that has done this," Ulrik agrees.

Ulrik's injury seems to be causing him significant discomfort. The colour has drained from him, making him look deathly pale.

"Ulrik, let me take a look at that wound," I say, moving towards him.

"I will be fine," he says through gritted teeth, grimacing as he brings his hand to his side. His right leg buckles, and Darmour swings in to catch him before he falls.

"Easy, captain." He helps Ulrik up the steps to the helm where he sits him down. "Zerina, you need to heal him."

Ulrik raises his tunic to reveal the puncture marks in his abdomen. They have worsened. Blackened veins track around the clawed gash and the wound itself is weeping, a green mucus coating the lacerations.

I place both my hands on his stomach, his skin burning to the touch. His wound is already ravaged with infection. "*Septum, mordu, tregu,*" I mutter the incantation over and over, channelling healing magic down my arms and onto the gashes. Ulrik grits his teeth, sweat beading on his ever-paling face. I pull my hands away only to see that the injury has worsened. The blackened veins have spread even further, the green mucus oozing from his skin. My heart sinks.

"What's wrong? Why does yer magic not heal him?" Darmour asks.

"I – I do not know." My hands tremble. I try another incantation. There is nothing in my mind that can guide me.

"Ulrik!" Esara's cries worsen as she forces her way forward to take hold of his hand. "Ulrik, don't do this to me! Not you too!"

"It will be okay, Esara. Everything will be okay. As long as you are safe. That is all that matters to me." Ulrik talks through laboured breaths as he struggles to form his words.

"He's lost a lot of blood. Zerina, there must be something ye can do?" Darmour asks. "Zerina!"

Darmour's words snap me back. "I cannot replace the blood that he has lost, and I am unable to seal his wound."

Darmour immediately applies pressure to Ulrik's wound. My eyes well with tears and I move towards Ulrik to bring him comfort. "Here, I can lessen the pain. That is all I can do."

"Zerina, promise me – I need you to promise to keep my sister safe." He is still fighting the pain, but my magic has at least brought him some comfort.

"Is this what you ask of me?" I squeeze his hand in my own, my cheeks burning with the tears I shed.

"I knew in this world, I would only be a spark. The spark that ignites the change that is needed. I have every faith you and Esara can make a difference in this world." Ulrik winces, his words becoming more and more difficult to muster.

"I promise I will do as you ask, Ulrik. I will keep her safe. No matter what."

"Thank you, Zerina, I appreciate everything you have done for us over these months, everything you have done for me. My sister is still free and that is down to you." Ulrik swallows hard before continuing. "Esara." His words are slowing. "I love you."

"I love you too, Ulrik." Esara only just manages her words.

Ulrik raises his hand and brushes away Esara's tears, holding her face. He smiles at her gently.

Then Ulrik's eyes close, and he takes his last breath.

"No no no no no, wake up Ulrik, you have to wake up!" Esara releases a shrill scream that pierces my ears.

Her brother is dead.

My heart breaks for the pain she is feeling, my heart breaks for the man I have come to love myself. I lose control and drop to my knees, burying my face into Ulrik as I scream out in anguish. The loss, the pain, the torment. How many times must we be forced to endure this in our lifetime? My throat burns as I scream. I am so angry at the gods of this world and the way they torment us.

All the magic in the world and there is nothing I can do to bring him back, to see him smile one last time.

I reach for Esara and bring her in close, and the two of us sob together, our hearts broken for the man we have lost.

"He was an honourable man and a great captain," says Darmour, and he salutes our fallen leader.

"Aye," Yigress and Marik call out in unison whilst also saluting.

Esara scrambles to her feet and runs towards the captain's quarters. She is inconsolable, but I follow her nonetheless. I promised Ulrik I would keep her safe no matter what, and this is now my duty.

"It's not fair, it isn't right. He was a good man, look at how the world treated him, look at the things he had to do to protect us because of them." Esara's grief is very quickly turning to anger.

"They need to pay. If not for what they did, we would have never set off on this stupid voyage, Ulrik would still be with us." Esara's eyes are red with tears, and she sobs in between her words. I worry that if she does not gather herself, she might faint.

"He was right." Esara begins to pace around the room.

"What do you mean?"

"I heard your conversation. I will make them pay for what they have done."

"Esara, Ulrik would not want you talking the lives of others in his name."

"Then we will use fear!" She stops in her tracks, as if her mind has a newfound sense of clarity. "That is what he said to you in this room, that the use of fear would aid in diplomacy."

I am unsure what to say.

"It is I that died on this day," says Esara through gritted teeth. "It is my name they will come to fear. And fear me they will."

She starts to summon her magic to a level I have not seen her wield before, and it frightens me. She grows taller as her appearance changes. I gasp when I see her brother standing before me.

Her anger is etched into his face, something I have not seen before. Now I understand what she asks. I have made a promise to Ulrik, to protect his sister no matter what. If this is how she wants to avenge him, then so be it.

She steps towards the door of the captain's quarters before turning to face me.

"They will fear us, and by the gods, I will make the king pay!"

# EPILOGUE

'The seas have never seen such a terrifying pirate, aided by one of the most powerful witches Levanthria has ever seen. His beard is as black as the night sky, but not as dark as his heart.

They rule the seas with fear. No one is brave enough to challenge his power. The ship that he captains, named after his fallen sister.

Heed my warning. If you see the blackened sails of Esara's Revenge, you do what you need to escape.'

-Message to the Vance Tyrain, Naval Commander of the King's Royal Fleet KR 860

# Also By

**The Levanthria Series**

A Forest Of Vanity And Valour

A Frost Of Fear And Fortitude - Pre Order

**The Spirit Beast Series**

Arnold Ethon And The Lions Of Tsavo

Arnold Ethon The Eagle And The Jaguar

Arnold Ethon And The War Of The Roses

# BE THE FIRST TO PRE-ORDER

A Kingdom Of Courage And Cruelty

The next epic story in the Levanthria series. Now carrying a curse that has transformed him into a lizard-man, Follow Orjan as he seeks to liberate the fallen kingdom of Eltera.

**ISBN:** 978-1-7398218-2-1
**Book Cover Design** - Rafido Digital Art

**Editing by Quill & Bone editing**
**https://www.quillandbone.com**

Published By A.P. Beswick Publications